THE DiAMOND DiSTRiCT

50 Cent

and

Derrick R. Pledger

G Unit
Books
New York   London   Toronto   Sydney

Pocket Books
A Division of Simon & Schuster, Inc.
1230 Avenue of the Americas
New York, NY 10020

First G-Unit/MTV/Pocket Books trade paperback edition March 2008

For information about special discounts for bulk purchases,
please contact Simon & Schuster Special Sales
at 1-800-456-6798 or business@simonandschuster.com.

Manufactured in the United States of America

10 9 8 7 6 5 4 3 2 1

ISBN-13: 978-1-4165-5179-9
ISBN-10:   1-4165-5179-4

To my younger brothers,

Akeen & Rashon

Success comes in many different shapes and sizes . . .

ACKNOWLEDGMENTS

Anything in this world is possible. I know this because the idea for this project was born while I was in Iraq working to protect my comrades from bombs and bullets. That was my mission. Now . . . 50 Cent, Pocket Books, myself, and the other talented authors involved with this publishing imprint are loyal to another mission. We are trying to combat the illiteracy epidemic plaguing American culture. The fact is our younger generation at large has less desire to be taught; they crave to be entertained. This is precisely why we must adapt and create savvy platforms to spread relevant messages to the masses.

Critics of the street-lit genre have been attempting to discredit this form of literature because it does not fit the traditional literary frameworks that have been around for decades. True enough, some of the stories are risqué; however, the intent is to emphasize the realities of an imperfect world as well as persuade folks to read who otherwise would never pick up a book. Interestingly enough, the same authors, journalists, and naysayers who criticize this genre should be thanking those of us who have produced a wider market that boasts thousands upon thousands of new readers. So on behalf of all hip-hop lit writers—you're all welcome.

To the many of you that have embraced this groundbreaking form of literature—I extend my sincere thanks. To everyone that has taken this ride with me, it's only right that I give you credit. None of this would have been possible without any you: 50 Cent, Marc Gerald, Lauren McKenna, Megan McKeever, Louise Burke, John Vairo Jr., Nikki Martin, G-Unit, and the entire Pocket Books staff. It is truly a privilege to have the opportunity to work with such seasoned professionals.

In closing, I give special thanks to my family, friends, and everyone that had influence on this journey: my wifey, the League, the "Owt" Team, and my hometown of Harrisburg, PA. This is only the beginning. . . .

—D.R.P.

ONE

As I hustled down the granite steps of Richardson Hall, it felt like the sun was shining brighter and the air smelled a little sweeter. My five-year stay at the University of Pennsylvania had finally come to a close.

College had always come easy to me, even though I wasn't really focused on what I should have been. I spent most of the time quenching my thirst for women instead of paying attention to my studies. I bet if you tested me on secrets to making a chick cum, I'd probably score a 99. As a result, my grades in college weren't stellar, but my experiences were priceless.

My mom was so excited that she almost swiped the curb as she pulled up. I knew that as soon as I hopped in the car, I'd be bombarded with the life questions. I'll be damned if that wasn't the first thing she brought up.

"Playtime is over now, honey . . . I hope you have a plan for what you are going to do with the rest of your life."

"How did I know that was going to be the first thing out of your mouth? Can I just enjoy the moment for once?" I asked.

Before she could respond, I decided to spill my intentions so she didn't start harassing me like some evil stepmother.

"My plan is to do the army thing for a few years and then head straight to law school so I can start making that Johnnie Cochran money."

"You would make a great lawyer, son," she said. "You have spent enough time talking those good girls out of their innocence. I'm sure you won't have too much trouble with a jury."

I guess she ignored the fact that I got my manipulative ways from her. We both thought that the world was one step behind us.

♦

There was heavy traffic on the way home. The trip usually took about two hours, but it ended up being close to three and a half this time. I didn't mind because we got a chance to bond and reminisce about the good ol' days.

We drove up to the front of the infamous split-level home—the nabe's party house—on the corner and I was surprised to see that there were only a few cars outside. My whole family had left my graduation early, but I thought everybody was going back to our house afterward. I was disappointed because I was looking forward to spending time with my folks.

I reluctantly opened up the front door and about thirty people yelled, "Congratulations!" I had a smile on my face from ear to ear despite the fact that I hated surprises. I briefly glanced at the dining room table and spotted a vast assortment of my favorite liquors, so I knew that it was going to be a long night.

My girl greeted me with a kiss and handed me another hefty bag of graduation gifts. I remember thinking, *Hell with the gifts, pass me a cold beer and a double shot.* I had a lot of love for her because she always took care of me. It didn't hurt that she was a brown-skinned, model-looking broad with long black hair and an ass that would make you do a triple take. Plenty dudes tried to wife her up back in the day, including me, but she wouldn't holla at me because she claimed I was a whore. I used to tell her that whores get paid for their services. I was different because I knocked down chicks for free.

Then years later, I ran into her at the West Mall off of Paxton Boulevard. I told myself at that moment she'd be my number one. I had no problem pushing every other female I had on my roster to the bench. I was used to juggling three, four, and five women at a time, but none of them ever compared to Tara.

I waltzed to the dining room table and poured myself a healthy shot of Patrón as I headed out back to the patio. I knew all my boys were out there because I heard them from outside, disturbing the peace as usual. As soon as I made my way out of the door, Dre staggered my way to give me a hug and almost stumbled to the ground. He was a real skinny dude who stood about six feet five inches, with arms that probably could reach his knees when he stood straight up. If you gave him just a few drinks, though, he'd be kissing the floor in no time.

The other goons I ran with growing up were there, too. My best friend Kevin, Fat Chris, and Joey, had all shown up. We called ourselves "the League" and that's how we were known around town. Harrisburg is a relatively small city nestled between Pittsburgh and Philly, but that didn't stop us planting our seeds from New

York to Florida. I surely wouldn't be surprised if one or two of us had a few bastards running around somewhere. We prided ourselves on doing anything that we pleased, regardless of who it offended. That's probably why we were hated by many and loved by few—unless you were female, of course. All of us had conflicting personalities, but we hung together because of the one thing we had in common—chasing women. None of us ever discriminated, either. If you had a phat ass, one of us was going to try you. It didn't matter if a chick looked like Rosie O'Donnell; somebody was still going to seize the moment. After all, it all looks and feels the same when the lights go out. At least that was how we used to justify sleeping with a beast.

"You know we're getting fucked up tonight, dog," Kev said.

"Yeah, and we ain't trying to hear that 'going back to college' shit because class is over, nigga," added Bum.

The binge drinking had begun.

"Stop talking and pour me another shot," I said. "I'll drink every one of y'all niggas under the table."

After killing about twenty shots of liquor and close to forty beers between us, we started making a lot of noise, so my mom got upset.

My house was the spot where we'd set up shop every weekend. It didn't matter whether it was a party or an orgy, she always felt better if we did it at the crib. She worried less knowing we were all safe, and being there also prevented us from drinking and driving, something that we did way too often.

We kept the party going until she couldn't take it anymore.

"D.J., y'all gonna have to take all that rowdy shit somewhere else," she hollered out of the kitchen window.

It was obvious that we had worn out our welcome. No matter, though, it was time for a change of scenery anyway, so we took the party to the streets.

TWO

We pulled into the parking lot of the Firefly two cars deep. I could tell that the spot was going to be packed because the lot was damn near full and it was still early.

The Firefly was the nightclub that everybody went to on Saturday nights. People hadn't seen the whole League together in a while, so I knew we were going to attract a lot of attention. As soon as we hopped out of the cars into the crowded parking lot, people began to notice.

"Is that D.J.?" a soft voice echoed behind us.

"Damn . . . can the nigga get into the club first? He just graduated today," Dre said in a slurred voice.

"Broke-ass niggas always got something smart to say," mumbled the girl.

"What, bitch?" Dre shouted.

He started to walk back toward her and before we knew it, he poured the rest of his beer all over her.

"Oh shit, he doused that bitch with his brew," Kev said, chuckling.

Everybody started laughing hysterically. The night had just begun and some crazy shit had already happened. I felt bad for her, but she looked like a pig with a ponytail so I didn't let it bother me. Joey was pissed, though, and he let his feelings be known.

"Dre, you always disrespecting broads! That's why you don't get no chicks now," Joey said heatedly.

He always tried to play the gentleman role. It wouldn't have been out of the ordinary for him to holla at a chick that just got showered by a beer like she had. That's just how thirsty he was for any broad with a wet kitty. He had no shame to his game. On one of our drunken nights, he let a freak suck his pipe after she hurled eight times, two of which were in his lap. If you ran with us, you were bound to see something extreme on the daily. Restraint was something that none of us seemed to understand for some reason.

We walked up to the front of the club only to be stalled by a long line. I was glad because we posted up on the picturesque wall so we could intercept any eye candy waiting to enter the club.

Suddenly, I heard somebody yell my name from somewhere in the crowd. Seconds later, one of my ex-high school flames strolled up with her best friend.

"What's good, D.J.?" she said. "I haven't seen you in a minute."

"Chillin', what's poppin' with you?" I replied.

"You still keeping your head in those books?" she uttered with an awkward smirk.

"Nah, shorty, I graduated earlier today."

"That's wussup," she said. "Maybe you, me, and my girl can celebrate later on tonight then."

"What you mean, 'celebrate'?" I said.

"Never mind, you probably can't handle both of us. I used to put your ass to sleep myself!"

"Imagine that," I snapped back.

I'm not even going to lie. This chick stayed wetter than Niagara Falls, so she definitely had me whipped for a few months. Before school, during school, after school, she was a real nympho in the flesh. She didn't go both ways then, but I was sure then that it was only going to be a matter of time before she crossed over.

The line began moving quick, so I kept the conversation to a minimum as we edged closer to the entrance. We breezed through security and finally made our way in. Just as I had suspected, it was packed like a can of sardines. All of us dispersed so we could mingle before meeting up at our table.

We always parlayed at the red velvet booth by the stairs so we could scheme on broads coming on and off the dance floor. Most folks didn't like sitting there because people were always getting too close to the table. The waitresses usually gave us free drinks when somebody bumped it and spilled something, so we didn't mind taking the risk. Finally, everybody sat down and began ordering drinks. Of course, Kev ordered a few bottles of top-shelf champagne and the most expensive liquor in the joint.

Kev was always trying to play the role, as if he had already attained celebrity status. It didn't matter, though, because he was going to the NFL soon, so he spent money like it was nothing. All of us teased him about his "wanna-be-a-baller" habits when we hit the clubs. This time was no different.

"Everywhere we go, you gotta be the one acting like

you're big business," said Fat Chris. "You gonna be broke before you even catch your first pass as a pro!"

"Hold up, my nigga. D.J. just graduated today, so we gonna do it big for him," said Kev. "Plus, I bet all y'all niggas try to sip my shit as soon as it gets here, so stop frontin'."

He was definitely right.

♦

As soon as the drinks came, the Moët was the first thing everyone reached for. I truly hated it when people chose a drink just because they saw it on a video or heard it in a song. To me, all of it tasted like cat piss anyway. I still poured myself a bubbly glass to chase the two shots of tequila I'd ordered, so I was just like everyone else.

It felt good to be back with the League. Everybody was having a good time hollering at all the broads and enjoying the atmosphere. Dre guzzled all his drinks quickly so he began talking bullshit, as usual.

"Y'all niggas be babysittin'. I'm going to get a couple more shots," he said. "Anybody want something?"

Everybody else was still sipping on their first round, so we all declined.

"Fuck it! I'll hit the bar by myself then," Dre uttered.

He posted up at the bar to wait for his poison instead

of coming back to the table. Dre was a sucker for light-skinned chicks, so when a badass redbone sat beside him he was in luck.

"What's good, cutie?" he asked.

"Trying to stay cool, it's hot as hell up in here," she responded.

"Why don't you let me buy you a margarita or something so you can cool off?"

"Do I look like a frozen-drink bitch to you?" she answered.

"My bad, shorty, get whatever you want then."

"I probably drink harder than you," she replied.

"I doubt it. I drink the finest of tequila . . . straight with no chaser."

"Yes, honey, I can kill a bottle of that myself!"

"Well, we might be a match made in heaven then, baby. I'm gonna get us two shots each so I can see if you're serious. Don't be writing checks that your ass can't cash."

"Please . . . you don't know who you messing with, boo," she returned.

He loved ghetto broads for some odd reason. Not that there is a problem with them, but it was just something that I never understood. That's why he had five kids and three baby mamas now. He must have talked the broad's panties back on because he was flirting for about thirty minutes. All he did was raise the price of pussy by making chicks feel all special. People like him messed it up for cats just trying to bang something after the club let out.

Back at the table, we were reminiscing about our younger days. Bum got angry because we kept teasing him about how ugly his main chick was. His broad looked like a dark-skinned Dave Chappelle, but she had money so he kept her around. She was more than horrible, but he still found it in his heart to deal with her. I would never want to wake up next to her, that's for sure.

Dre came back and started telling us how he had just secured his victim for the night.

"Awwww shit, nine months from now, this nigga gonna have another nappy-headed baby boy," Fat Chris said jokingly.

"Fuck you, fat boy! You wish you could hit as many bitches as I have," barked Dre.

All of us argued back and forth like this on the daily. We had each other's backs regardless, though. That's why I loved every last one of them.

The club closed at two o'clock, but we stepped outside fifteen minutes early. There was already a crowd of people posted up on their vehicles near the entrance.

These fools thought they were in a music video, too. We gathered near the door so we could monitor who was coming out. It was time for us to track down something to go home with. I already knew what I wanted to get into. I just had to find those two freaks who had rolled up on me earlier.

Just then, two guys approached us who didn't seem to be too happy. It was weird because they were both well dressed and had jewelry flashing from head to toe. They didn't seem like the type of cats who really wanted to cause any drama, but when they started talking shit, it was obvious that's what they had come for.

"Which one of y'all bitch niggas poured a beer on my girl?" one of them asked.

This was the wrong night for somebody to be popping off at the mouth. My whole squad was drunk, so it was just an invitation for something tragic.

"I did, pussy, and I will pour one on you, too," Dre said.

"Bring your ass around the corner then, you bitch-ass nigga," he replied.

He wasn't a small dude, so I was hoping Dre didn't get his ass beat down. It's not like we would have let that happen, but I was still a little worried.

As soon as Dre got around the corner, he swung on

him and they started tussling. Kev and Bum watched for about thirty seconds, then jumped in and wrestled him to the ground. His white linen suit became decorated with black scuff marks in no time.

Meanwhile, Fat Chris and Joey took care of his accomplice. I felt bad because both these jokers were getting their asses whipped in front of everybody. My boys must have stomped these clowns for about five minutes until the bouncers came around the corner to break it up.

By that time, Joey and I had already gotten the cars and were yelling for the others to hop in.

"Let's fuckin' go! The cops are probably on their way right now," I screamed.

Dre and Kev jumped in my ride, laughing uncontrollably.

"Y'all are some dickheads. Every time we go out, some dumb shit always happens."

"Stop crying, nigga, you ain't up at college no more. This is how shit goes down in the 'hood, or did you forget?" Dre said. "Don't act like we never beat a nigga down back in the day!"

It didn't matter where it was. These dudes always stumbled into trouble like it came looking for them. It was as if starting some shit was on their to-do list every weekend and I was always forced to participate. That's just how goons in the League operated. I had just graduated that day, so there was no way that I was fighting or getting into any other drama.

We argued for a few, but eventually got off the subject. I dropped Kev off at some chick's house across the river and kept moving. Dre and I were the only ones still hanging out.

"Which one of your baby mamas you want to see tonight?" I asked Dre.

"Fuck all three of them, dog. Drop me off at the Waffle House. That honey I bagged at the club is meeting me there at three."

"Shorty probably ain't even gonna show up," I replied.

About ten minutes later, we pulled up to the Waffle House, where everybody eats after the club lets out.

"Good lookin', dog," he said as he got out of the car. "Oh, I almost forgot. Congratulations! I'm proud of you, dog. Oh, before I forget . . . I got something for you, too."

He reached into his back pocket and pulled out two watches, a necklace laced with a Jesus charm as big as my fist, and a diamond-studded bracelet. It felt like a ten-pound baby when he tossed everything onto my lap. I didn't know that he had taken their jewelry, too.

"You a fool for that, nigga," I uttered. "Now instead of assault and battery, you gonna get a robbery charge, too."

"Fuck them bitch-ass niggas," he mumbled as he walked up to the Waffle House entrance.

I told him to call my cell if he needed me and then I drove off. I could feel myself swerving all the way back to the house. I shouldn't have driven home. It was truly by the grace of God that I made it.

THREE

I woke up Sunday morning with a throbbing headache that made me feel like I was one of the dudes that my boys destroyed the night before. It was almost noon and I was still tipsy. I tried to sneak out of the bed, but Tara was already awake, too.

"How many of those scandalous bitches tried to holla at you last night?" she asked in a groggy voice.

"Nobody tried to holla at me, I was chillin' with my boys all night," I replied.

In the back of my mind, I was thinking that if I would have found those two chicks that approached me before going in the club, I would have had my way with both of them.

"Whatever, D.J.," she said as she sat up.

Tara was far from a fool, so she knew how I got down when I came home. She didn't care about the girls that I had up at school because she never had to face them. However, she didn't want me fooling with broads close to home because she hated grimy chicks who smiled in her face but were trying to give me their goods behind her back.

She knew I had a surplus of freaks, but as long as it didn't interfere with us, she wouldn't mention it. Every man wishes his girl was the same.

I hopped in the shower so I could get ready for another day on the town. I felt a sudden wave of relief as the hot water pounded my face. As I was rinsing, I heard the door close lightly, so I peeped outside the curtain to see what was going on. Tara was standing next to the mirror naked as a newborn.

"What you doing, Tara?"

"Minding my business," she replied.

She had been a smart-ass her entire life. That's why everybody always thought she was so stuck-up. She jumped in the shower with me and started kissing in all the right places. It didn't take long for my manhood to rise to the occasion. We went at it for about ten minutes until I heard my little brothers giggling outside the door. I'm sure they knew what was going on.

After our wet 'n' wild session, we patrolled back into my room so I could get dressed. I had six missed calls on my cell phone, so I knew my boys were ready to get it started again. I peeked over and Tara was already sleeping like a baby. That meant I'd handled my business.

As I was walking out the door, I glanced at my dresser and saw the jewelry that Dre had seized from the guys at the club.

What am I going to do with this shit, I asked myself.

I was no fan of gaudy jewelry, so I knew I wasn't going to wear any of it. Besides, I had always thought dudes who ran around wearing all types of "bling" just to show off were clowns.

This shit is probably fake anyway, I thought.

♦

I headed to the West Mall so I could cop something to wear. I didn't feel complete unless I had on a fresh knit and a pair of white Air Force Ones. I wanted to stop past my friend Tony's jewelry spot, too, so I could see how much the things Dre gave me were worth.

Tony was the fast-talking, mob-affiliated guy who

owned the Diamond District. Everybody in the city went to him for all their jewelry needs. We always called him "Yacob the Jeweler" because he used to say that his inventory was better than that of the real Jacob the Jeweler, who happens to be the supplier for rich folks. I wasn't into jewelry, so it really didn't matter how quality his "ice" was. I got my gear straight and headed downstairs to the District.

As I walked in, I noticed that there was only one other person at the counter, so I was right on time.

"What's good, Tony Macaroni?" I said. "Why don't you and those mob niggas stop smuggling drugs and jewelry into the States?"

"Where you been at, college boy?" asked Tony.

"That college shit is officially over! I graduated yesterday," I replied.

"Congratulations," he said in his hard, Italian accent.

You could tell that he was connected for real. This whole jewelry business was a front for something much bigger. I just couldn't figure out what else he was into.

"I came up on some merchandise and I want you to let me know what it's worth," I said in a very low voice.

"Let's see what you got," he countered.

I pulled out the jewels and gently positioned them on the counter.

"Who did you rob? Probably some rapper, huh?" Tony asked.

"Nah, one of my friends is real heavy into jewelry and this is all his old stuff. He gave it to me as a graduation present," I explained.

"I'll be right back. I have to step in the back to see if this shit is authentic. I hope you didn't bring me some costume jewelry," he added.

I sat down in one of the red leather couches in the shop so I could wait for him. About fifteen minutes passed, so I started to get restless.

"Yo, TONEEYYY," I shouted.

He came out of the back with a huge smile on his face.

"What you smiling at?" I asked. "Was the shit fake or something?"

"Your boy must have a little bit of money, huh?"

"What makes you say that?" I said.

"I can resell all of these things for about fifteen or sixteen thousand," he answered.

Before I could say anything, he told me to meet him at his car in the back parking lot in ten minutes.

His ride was easy to spot because he was the only cat with a red Porsche that said ROC HARD on the license plate. He strolled up to the car and hopped in with a black tote bag in his left hand.

"I think if we work together, we can make some serious money," he said.

"I don't want to be a part of any of that illegal shit you and your people are into. Y'all about to get caught soon anyway," I said jokingly.

"Well, catch this," he said with a very serious look on his face.

He tossed the black bag that he was gripping into my lap. He gazed at me with a piercing look as if he wanted me to open it. I was shocked by what I saw.

"What the fuck? What's all this?" I asked.

I pulled out a stack of fifty- and hundred-dollar bills in disbelief.

"It's eight thousand in cash and there is more where that came from if we can work this thing out."

I couldn't believe that he had just slapped eight grand into my lap.

"All you have to do is keep bringing me expensive goods that I can resell or melt down to make new pieces," Tony said. "I will give you fifty percent of what everything is worth as long as you bring me quality."

For stacks like he had just given me, I would have brought him anything he asked for.

I had a million and one thoughts running through my head at that moment. The main thing I was considering was how I was going to spend all the money. My brainstorming was quickly interrupted by Tony's voice.

"You act like you never saw a few grand before," Tony exclaimed.

I had hustled a little weed back in the day, so I was used to handling two or three stacks at once, but eight thousand cash was a different ball game, at least for me.

"C'mon, Tony, I was just thinking about ways to come up on more jewels for you," I said.

"You are a smart li'l college nigga, so I am sure you'll figure it out," he said.

"Watch your fuckin' mouth, dog! You cool, but don't be dropping N-bombs in my presence," I replied. "You don't know shit about the black struggle . . . ain't no niggas in Italy," I said grudgingly.

"Just come back and see me when you got some more bling and I will take care of you," he uttered.

We slapped hands and I hopped out of the car, holding the black bag tightly. I parked in the front of the mall so I had to hike around the entire building. That's when the lightbulb in my head went off.

I hit Dre on his cell and let him know that I had a surprise for everybody. I told him to gather the League and meet me at the crib ASAP.

About forty-five minutes later, Dre and the rest of my boys were waiting for me when I arrived at my house. They had no idea what I had in store for them.

FOUR

I hobbled out onto the patio with a cooler full of Heineken. This was the first time that they didn't rush me as I brought beer out to the chill spot.

"What's the big surprise, dog?" Kev asked.

"He probably getting married or some gay shit like that," Fat Chris followed sarcastically.

"Nah, fat boy, I'm married to this money I'm about to pass out," I said. "You should be thanking me right now."

I threw a thousand-dollar wad of cash to each of them. There has never been a time when I could get the four of these dudes to shut up all at once. I guess I had their attention this time. Joey was the first one to say something.

"I know you ain't about any illegal shit, so where did you get all this cash?"

"I know, right . . . this nigga has never even got a parking ticket," followed Fat Chris.

"I guess I learned something in college after all," I said.

"What the fuck, dog? Stop playin' games! Where did you get all this bread?" Kev asked seriously.

"If y'all stop yappin', I will tell you how we can make more than this little chump change," I replied.

Everybody was all ears. Of course they were paying much attention. Who wouldn't after somebody just passed out four grand in cash? I kept the other four thousand for myself. After all, I was the one who made moves to get the money. Most people wouldn't have parted with any of the cash, to be realistic. Truthfully, I needed them, and that's why I had to spread the wealth.

I gave them a quick rundown of how the operation would work, but I purposely left out some of the details.

"The more ice I take to my connection, the more cash I can spread between the League," I explained.

"There is gonna be a whole lot of niggas missing they jewels. I'm gonna go on a hella robbing spree," said Dre.

This idea was right up his alley. Dre had been carrying pistols around since we were in ninth grade and he was definitely no stranger to robbery.

"So you telling me that all we have to do is rob people for they jewels and give them to you?" Fat Chris asked.

"It's that simple," I said. "It doesn't matter what you do to get it. The bottom line is more jewelry equals more cash."

For a split second, I asked myself if I should have even turned over this stone. It was too late now, though. Everybody was hungry and willing to do whatever it took to make more money.

We spent about an hour discussing the best places to get more jewels without taking a lot of risks. Dre felt like he had to be in control since he was a self-proclaimed stick-up artist. It was no secret that he was a predicate felon, but he made sure that everybody knew it.

"I got a couple extra guns at one of my baby mom's house that I can give y'all niggas," Dre said.

"I know the perfect spots where we can go handle business, too," said Chris.

"No doubt! All we gotta do is snatch niggas up coming out of the clubs, just like the other night. Fools trying to stunt make easy targets," said Dre.

"Shit . . . we should just rob Kev for his watch and chain . . . let's start with him," joked Joey.

"Yeah, right. Y'all niggas ain't taking shit from me."

I could tell they were getting way too anxious. I let them know up front that I wasn't taking part in any robberies whatsoever. I was no fan of taking things from people that didn't belong to me. Then again, I was encouraging them to do so.

For the next couple hours, we solidified our plans as to how we were going to get the most jewelry in the shortest amount of time. The afternoon was drawing to a close and Tara kept peeking out of the door. It was about time for us to rap things up.

"Don't spend all your dough in one place," I said.

"Fuck spending, the robbin' spree starts tonight," announced Dre. "Me and Chris are about to hit the streets as soon as we get outta here."

"Y'all niggas be safe," I said. "I'm chillin' with the wifey tonight." Tara came outside and sat on my lap, so they knew it was time to go.

"Leave so I can have some time with my man," she said. "I'm starting to think y'all are gay."

"Tell your friend Ashley to come through and holla

at me. I'll show her just how gay I am," huffed Kev. "She owes me anyway."

"She got what she wanted," Tara said playfully. "She told me that you knew how to work your tongue, but not good enough to let you have the rest of the goodies."

"D.J., you need to check your girl, dog! She's outta pocket talking that dumb shit," Kev murmured as he began walking down the patio steps.

"I ain't got nothing to do with it," I replied. "Dre and Chris, y'all dudes be safe. Hit me up later when you're through."

"No doubt."

The day had finally started to wind down. It had been a long but productive weekend. Graduation, friends, family, and eight grand mixed together made life seem almost surreal for a moment.

Little did I know . . . my perfect world would change as we edged deeper into the summer.

FIVE

It was Thursday evening and I hadn't heard anything from Dre or the rest of the League in a few days. Friday was close, which meant they would be calling soon so we could figure out our plans for the weekend.

I had been spending time with Tara all week so when the weekend did come, I could be in the streets without her complaining. We went on a few shopping sprees and I was curious why she hadn't asked me where I had gotten all the money I was spending. Then I remembered that I had scored almost two grand for graduation, so I assumed that's where she thought the cash was coming from.

Where it came from was irrelevant to her because she was the one that was reaping the reward. I bought her a couple pair of Louis Vuitton shoes, a matching handbag, and something else from every female store we went into.

Hell, I even paid for a day of pampering at the spa for her. The funny thing is, when I tried to drop her off, she forced me to come in, too. She didn't want me to leave, so I did the whole spa thing with her. I felt metrosexual as hell. I always thought a male who goes to a spa was on some homosexual shit. Still, I felt so good after my Swedish massage was over that I wanted to make another appointment, but my pride wouldn't allow it.

At about ten thirty that night, I heard someone knocking on the back door. I already knew it was one of my boys because they were the only ones who weren't afraid of my little brother's pit bull in the backyard. I scurried to the patio and saw that they had already come in and raided the fridge.

"Ain't this a bitch! Y'all niggas act like you live here," I said sternly.

"You know we all family," Dre replied.

Dre, Kev, and Fat Chris were sitting at the table already.

"Take a seat so I can show you what Santa and his little dwarfs brought home."

"Elves, you dumb-ass nigga! Santa's helpers are called elves," Kev said mockingly. "How the fuck you mix up Santa Claus with Snow White?"

"Fuck you, Santa, and his elves," countered Dre.

I really didn't feel like hearing all the bickering and bullshitting. They sounded like two bad-ass kids arguing over whose mom was fatter. It was getting late and I had been running around all day.

"What's the deal?" I asked. "What y'all got to show me?"

Kev and Fat Chris simultaneously shifted their attention toward Dre. He took a book bag from behind his chair and handed it to me. It felt like he had a twenty-five-pound dumbbell in it or something.

I poured out the contents on the table as I glanced at him. He had a devilish smile on his face that I can remember like it was yesterday.

"How much cash you think your connection will give you for all this?" Kev asked.

"I'm not sure. He's particular about the kind of product he wants," I answered.

But in my mind I was thinking, *Holy shit!*

I couldn't believe how much jewelry they had con-fiscated.

"How many people did y'all rob?" I asked.

"We went to Philly and ran up on some broad who told us all the spots where a lot of hustlers hang out," said Fat Chris. "It was so many niggas rocking jewels downtown that we only had to stop on two strips."

"We took turns running up on niggas with the heat," said Dre excitedly. "They knew we were about busi-ness as soon as I flashed the sawed-off shotgun at them. That's when they would just start giving up everything they had. One nigga offered me a Whopper from Burger King and his money, too!"

"No shit," I replied.

"I was hungry as hell so I was like, fuck it," he con-tinued.

Dre never ceased to amaze me. He didn't have to take the man's food, too. He was truly a devious individual.

"What fucked me up is that the person who gave us the most trouble was a bitch," uttered Chris. "I thought I was gonna have to shoot this chick."

"Y'all niggas were robbing females, too?" Kev asked surprisingly.

"Is a green bean fuckin' green?" said Dre. "What

makes you think a bitch can't get robbed? If I see a broad shining, I'm taking her diamonds and her phone number, too, nigga!"

"Y'all some grimy dudes," I said, chuckling.

Fat Chris was kind of a rough dude, but Dre was really an animal. He didn't care about anything or anybody, except for us and maybe his kids when he wasn't arguing with their mothers.

"Here's the deal," I said. "I'm gonna take this shit to my connection tomorrow and see what we get."

"Don't try to skip town with the dough," joked Kev.

"Shut that dumb shit up," I replied. "Y'all might rob me before I can even split the money up!"

I was joking, but when a large sum of cash was on the line, people's true colors started showing.

"I'm gonna go ahead and lay it down for the night," I said, yawning. "Meet me here around three thirty tomorrow so I can split the cash up. Clean up your fuckin' beer bottles, too! This ain't the Firefly," I commanded.

"We got it," said Dre. "Go in . . . go in the house with your pussy-whipped ass," he said as he choked off his beer.

I headed back upstairs to jump in the bed with Tara. I thought I was going to be able to see some action, but she was sound asleep, so I just let her relax. As I was trying to fall asleep, all I could think about was getting back to the Diamond District and the money I could make. Those thoughts were quickly replaced by a spell of anxiety. I felt like I had the devil on one shoulder and an angel on the other. I knew I had started something that could potentially have an ugly ending. This type of thing was certainly not up my alley and it was unquestionably illegal.

Fuck it. A couple grand in my pocket won't hurt, I thought as my eyes finally shut.

I had just spent almost five years busting my ass in college. Well, maybe not busting my ass, but at least I had graduated. There was no way that I wasn't going to enjoy my summer and having a job was not part of the plan. This seemed like the only way I could make this happen.

The devil had won.

SIX

The next morning, I woke up bright and early. After tossing and turning all night, I suppose I might have felt tired, but I felt better than ever. I followed Tara out as she left for work and then headed straight for the District. I figured it was early so he wouldn't have too many customers in his shop.

"What you got for me today, D.J., or should I call you 'Kanye,'" Tony asked as I walked in.

"Chill with all them Kanye jokes. All of a sudden, every nigga from the block that goes to college gotta be on some Kanye West shit," I said as I tossed the book bag on the glass counter.

"Damn, what you got up in here . . . a dead body, bro?"

"I told you I was gonna be coming through heavy," I replied.

"You know the routine . . . I have to go to the back room," he said. "Here are the keys to the Porsche. Don't even think about taking a joyride, either!"

I laughed and made my way to the back parking lot. When I turned on the engine, it sounded like I was at the Daytona 500. If I wasn't so worried about getting paid, I would have taken his Porsche for a spin. I remember being surprised because he had 50 Cent banging in his ride. Ironically, he probably couldn't even point out 50 or anyone else in the Unit if they walked in his store posing as a customer.

Tony finally came out about twenty minutes later. I made it a point to watch the mall entrance to make sure he had some cash in his hand. He didn't have a little black tote bag, though. He was carrying the book bag that I'd brought him the jewels in on his back.

He jumped in the driver's side and tossed it toward me.

"What you trying to do, break me?" he asked.

"What you mean?" I responded.

"Open up the bag and start counting," he said. "Time is money!"

I started to unravel the rolls of hundred-dollar bills so I could count the cash. I had never imagined that I would be holding this much bread at once.

"You are taking too long! I can see that you are not used to handling a lot of green," Tony said.

"What the fuck?" I replied abruptly. "You think I run around with thousands of dollars in cash on the regular?"

"Forget about it," he said roughly. "Don't worry about counting the money. I even put a little extra in for you. The four-karat diamond you brought was what put you over the top," he followed.

That was the ring that Fat Chris had taken from the female he had robbed.

"What do you mean, extra?" I asked.

"I only owed you eighteen grand, but I put twenty in the bag to make it even."

I couldn't believe this shit. Twenty thousand dollars? This hustle was way too easy.

"Next time you come see me, I'm gonna subtract two grand from what I owe you."

It didn't matter what he did next time. All I was worried about was the twenty stacks I had looking me in my face at that moment.

I began wondering what type of dude keeps this much cash stashed at his place of business. This just validated my suspicion that Tony was really into some big-money businesses—both legal and illegal.

"I better be able to sell some of the shit you brought me," he said. "I'm sure one of my clients will want something custom-made, so I will melt a lot of this down and make some tight pieces for them."

He might as well have been speaking Greek to me. The only thing on my mind was the twenty grand.

I couldn't wait to call the League to let them know the score. I came back down to earth and told Tony that I would make a drop every Friday or Saturday. I just wanted to get the money out of there as quickly as possible.

"You be safe out there, homey," he said.

"No doubt, it's been nice doing business with you," I replied.

"I'll see you next week."

I hopped out of the car with a death grip on the book bag. It was only about ten o'clock in morning so I had all day to burn.

It was time to splurge.

SEVEN

On the way home, my trunk looked as if I had just gone Christmas shopping. I copped some things for my mom, Tara, both my brothers, and of course for myself. For a brief moment, I contemplated what I would do if the cops pulled me over and discovered all the cash that I was riding with. They would have surely assumed me to be a drug runner or something of the sort. I wasn't the one robbing folks or doing anything illegal, though. My friends were doing all the dirty work. I was just the Good Samaritan who turned hard work and jewels into cash. Looking back, it was obvious that my thought process was totally warped.

It was about two thirty when I pulled up to the crib and my boys were already there, which did not surprise me. They rushed me as I hopped out of the car.

"Niggas show up late to work daily, but no one is ever late on payday," I said sarcastically.

I told them to meet me on the back porch in a few minutes so I could run in the house beforehand.

"Hurry up, nigga," Dre said, "it's time to get paid!"

I had to go in the house so I could take my share of the money off the top. These fools had no clue what type of bank I was getting from Tony. I didn't feel guilty taking a bigger cut because I was still putting money into all their pockets.

I decided that I was going to give each one of them three grand and keep eight for myself. Three stacks was a good payday for all of them. *Most people in America don't even make that in a month*, I thought. They wouldn't be getting anything if it wasn't for me, anyway.

I slid to the back porch after I had wrapped four bundles of three thousand dollars into separate rubber bands. They were all on the patio, waiting anxiously for my arrival.

"Not many bosses take care of his employees like I do," I said. "Here are your bundles."

"Since you the boss, D.J., where the fuck is my

medical benefits?" Dre replied. "I got kids to take care of."

"Shit, you better take your seeds to the free clinic," said Kev. "You go there once a month to get some gonorrhea and chlamydia pills, nigga."

We all bugged out when Kev said that. In reality, Dre did catch a few unwanted ailments in his days. When you hit as many chicks as he did, you were bound to catch something sooner or later; the fact that he didn't believe in condoms was the real problem.

"It's Friday night and all of us got big pockets," Joey said. "What y'all trying to get into tonight?"

"It's whatever for me, Kev, and Dre," I answered. "But you and Chris have to ask your girls if you can go out tonight. I know y'all niggas don't run your programs."

"And you run yours," a soft voice said from behind me.

I didn't know Tara was standing to my rear. She must have just crept in from work.

"Baby, don't front! You know I wear the boots in this relationship," I continued. "Now go get us a couple cold brews before I get mad."

"Whatever," she replied snidely.

"It don't seem like you run shit," said Fat Chris.

Two minutes later, Tara brought out a twelve-pack of Corona for us. That wasn't one of our beers of choice, but it still hit the spot. We were probably the dumbasses that kept the beer distributor around our way in business.

"Like I said, I run my program," I said confidently. "Thank you, baby . . . I have something for you later on since you've been good!"

We chilled for about an hour and decided to hit the streets shortly after. It was Friday so the club was going to be one of the spots where we definitely had to make an appearance.

The routine was the same for the next five or six weeks. My boys would take road trips to different places, robbing anyone they could. Next, they'd bring me everything they retrieved unless one of them really liked a piece. If that was the case, they'd just keep it. It didn't matter either way because if they wanted to get paid, all of them knew what was necessary. On weekends, I would go make a drop at the District and split the cash up soon after.

As time progressed, the internal battle I was facing raged on. I kept finding ways to justify everything that we were doing—even if the justifications were superficial or simply a bunch of bullshit. Sometimes I felt as if

I had been taking advantage of my friends to an extent, but all of us were enjoying the benefits of the operation. Everybody was content, not just me.

We were buying anything and everything we desired. I had unintentionally found myself in the center of a moneymaking juggernaut that was profiting thousands weekly.

Life was good. Life was real good.

EIGHT

I guess the old saying "Time flies when you're having fun" is the truth. It was almost the end of July, which meant two things: My birthday was around the corner and summer was in full bloom.

On the morning of my birthday, I picked up Kev at about eleven o'clock. We were going down to the Wheel Warehouse to cop some new rims for both of our cars. It was about ninety degrees and the city streets were already buzzing.

"It's some sexy bitches out here today, dog! I need to

add a few to my roster, too," said Kev as he anxiously gazed up and down the street.

"I don't see how you have time to spend with Dawn when you fucking with so many other freaks," I replied.

"It's all about balance and making sure these chicks stay in their lane. I'll teach you how to do it one day," he uttered.

"Nigga, everything you know you learned from me. I was the one who taught you the ropes of this shit," I contended.

I met Kev in the summer leading up to my senior year of high school. He wasn't the most popular dude, but he was always down for whatever. I took him on a set with two Catholic school broads out in the 'burbs by my house and we have been hanging tough ever since. Most people wouldn't believe some of the sexcapades we've participated in since we first started running together.

I dropped Kev off at his car, which he had left at his girl's house, and continued to the rim shop. There was a huge trailer parked in front of the spot so I was sure that they were getting some new inventory. I wanted to buy something exclusive that nobody else in the city would have.

"Can I help you?" the funny-looking clerk asked.

I guess he was going for a Gothic look. I could understand the dark clothing and eyeliner, but the trench coat in the middle of the summer was a bit over the top.

"We just browsing," Kev answered.

They had all of the new rims leaned up against the back wall, so that's the direction I went. At that time, I had a maroon Cadillac STS, so I needed something that was both big and classy. Kev had a 2005 Maxima with two twelve-inch woofers in it that you could hear two miles away.

"Yo, D.J., these joints will look hard on the Caddie, dog," said Kev.

"Nigga, you can't put them big-ass rims on a Cadillac. They are way too husky," I replied. "The largest I can go are nineteens."

"Well, hurry up, nigga, I already picked mine out," he said.

I kept looking for a while before I spotted a pair of eighteen-inch Lexanis that I knew would look tough on my vehicle.

"Gimme these, and four low-pro tires to match," I told the clerk.

"How would you like to pay? You can sign up for

our finance program today and receive ten percent off," he explained.

"Nah, homey, I'm paying cash," I said.

"You're paying cash?" he repeated with his eyebrows flared.

"Did I stutter, Marilyn Manson? Just tell me how much I owe and put my rims on," I said irritably.

I don't think he liked it when I pulled out $6,800 in cash and dropped it on the counter. Kev paid for his in cash, too, and we parlayed out front until they put our rims and tires on. They finished both cars in about an hour, so we cut around back to watch as they pulled them out of the garage.

"The Caddie is looking real thorough, my nigga," said Kev.

"Shit, the Maxima is killing it, too," I replied. "What's the deal now? It's my birthday, but I don't feel like going to hang with Tara just yet."

"Fuck hangin' with Tara today," he returned. "We already got a surprise for you, dog."

I had no idea what the surprise was. Usually, none of my boys could keep a secret, but I guess they succeeded this time. We decided to hit the car wash before we made our way to our destination. I couldn't ride on new rims without my car being as clean as a whistle.

"I know you ain't gonna run your shit through the automatic wash," I said as I shoved a five-dollar bill into the change machine.

"Why not, nigga? That's what it's for," he replied.

"Y'all dudes don't know how to take care of a car," I countered. "You have to treat them good and they will be good to you. Your shit probably gonna break down soon!"

"Speaking of breaking . . . don't you gotta break bread with the team today? I know you went to see the jewelry cat yesterday."

"Yeah, I did," I mumbled. "I wanna holla at y'all niggas about this whole situation. I don't think I can keep doing this shit, dog."

"What?" shouted Kev. "Nigga, what you trying to stop for now?"

"You and I both know that this shit can't go on forever," I said morbidly. "Besides, things are starting to get hot. There are people that know what's going down . . . I'm sure of it."

"I feel you," said Kev. "Just know that Dre and them ain't gonna be hearing all that. They like getting their money this way. It's too easy."

"That's why I want you to talk to them, too," I pleaded. "It needs to come from more than just me. We made a lot more dough than any of us imagined we would. I'm about done with shit, though . . . for real."

"That's fine, nigga," he replied. "But fuck all that right now. It's your birthday and we gonna do it like we supposed to. Hurry up so you can follow me."

♦

We took about twenty minutes to finish up the cars and continued on our way. As I followed Kev through the city, I decided that maybe it was not the best day to discuss ending the operation. After all, July 21 only came once a year. I was determined to enjoy myself, but I knew I couldn't keep my mouth shut about how I was feeling much longer. I was beginning to drive myself crazy.

NINE

When we pulled up to Beverly Park, it was already pretty crowded. I didn't think all these people were there for me until I saw a big sign that said "HAPPY B-DAY D.J." It was so many girls out there in booty shorts and bikini tops that I swore I was in heaven. I couldn't wait to see them all strip down.

I marched over to the pavilion because I spotted smoke coming from a grill and I was hungry as a hostage. To my surprise, the most unlikely person you could think of was actually doing the cooking.

"What the fuck you doing on the grill, Dre?" I asked.

"Happy birthday, my nigga! I'm like George Fore-man out on this muthafucka, dog," he responded. "It's packed out here, huh?"

"Yeah, it's definitely poppin'," I replied. "Who the hell are all these people?"

"I don't really know," he returned. "We just put the word out that the League would be giving out free food and free beer at Beverly Park. We knew that people would show up. Niggas always down for something free."

"Ain't that the truth!"

"Here, you can have this plate. There's ice-cold brew stocked in those big orange tubs by the tables, too."

As I sat there with Dre, we had probably talked about every chick that was out there and what we would do to every last one of them.

"Good look on the food. I'm gonna mingle for a little bit, but I have to talk to all y'all niggas later. It's impor-tant, so don't go far," I uttered.

I was surprised that I ate two plates. The food was actually good. I should have asked Dre how a dude that was supposed to be so "gangsta" could cook like a housewife.

As I surveyed the crowd for a second, I realized that there weren't many people I recognized. Some faces looked familiar but I couldn't put a finger on anyone I knew. I did spot the rest of my boys and a few broads chilling at a table by the pool, though. I crept up from behind so they didn't know I was coming.

"Oh shit, where you come from, nigga?" Fat Chris asked.

"You know me . . . I have been known to creep up on niggas," I replied.

"Well, I got something for you to creep up on right now," he said. "This is Maria."

"She is your birthday present from the League," Joey said as he marveled at her cleavage.

If you looked Maria up and down just a few times, there was no way you could really appreciate how sexy she was. You had to stare to actually comprehend her beauty. She was mixed with black and Filipino, so long curly hair and a caramel complexion were a given. Her body was ridiculous, too. If I were them, I would have been selfish as hell with her. Come to find out, she was the one who wanted to holla at me, so I guess they had no choice but to pass her on.

"Damn, Maria, this birthday keeps getting better and better with every minute," I said anxiously. "First new rims for my ride and now you," I added. "This day might go down in history."

"I heard you got a wifey, though. That's just too bad. I was looking forward to fulfilling your birthday wishes," she said, smiling.

"What makes you think you can't?" I replied.

"Because I don't break up happy homes," she answered.

"There's nothing wrong with getting to know a new face," I said. "How about you come take a ride with me? I have to run a quick errand."

"Your friends aren't going to get mad?"

"They could care less about me. All they're worried about is taking one of your girls home."

♦

We walked back over to the parking lot toward my car. I stayed a few paces behind her so I could stare at her Coke-bottle frame. This broad was truly a walking masterpiece. We finally got to my car where I opened the passenger-side door for her so she could slide in.

"Let me find out that you are a gentleman and a cutie, too," she said excitedly. "I might have to steal you from that girlfriend of yours after all."

"I thought you said you don't break up happy homes," I replied.

"If I want somebody, I do whatever it takes to get

them. I just don't like my business in the street," she whispered in a seductive voice.

When she said that, I immediately knew I was going to try her. I didn't have anything to lose anyway. Plus, there were fifty more broads out there waiting for me if she turned me down. The crazy thing was that I didn't even have to make a move. She leaned over and started kissing on my neck and rubbing me through my jeans. I turned on the car and the air conditioner because I figured we might be there for a while.

"How come you won't kiss me back?" she asked.

I usually wasn't a big kisser, but as sexy as this chick was, I didn't mind breaking the rules. We massaged lips for a few minutes as she unbuckled my pants. It was broad daylight outside but my tint was so dark that it didn't matter if people were looking. They couldn't see anyway.

"Pull it out," she whispered softly.

"Don't start something you can't finish," I replied.

By this point, my stick was already reaching for the sky. She kissed me on the lips one more time and then diverted her attention to my lap. The truth be told, she definitely handled her business like a professional. All I could do was grab the steering wheel to keep from squealing like a little girl. About twenty minutes was all I could handle. I had to lean back in the seat so I could get my mind together when she was finished.

"Happy birthday, sweetie," she said joyfully.

I didn't have the words to respond, so I just nodded my head and smiled.

"I thought you had some places you had to go," she murmured.

"Not anymore," I said. "I'm good. You made me forget what I wanted to do anyway!"

"I guess you enjoyed yourself then," she replied.

She pulled down the mirror so she could fix herself up and reapply her lip gloss. I was in awe because she was still looking perfect after she had just supplied me with her lip service. We made small talk for a little while longer before we decided to rejoin the party.

We scooted back over to the table and it was easy to see that everybody was tipsy. The four of my boys and the three of her friends were playing high-low, which was a drinking game that we used to loosen broads up before we went in for the kill.

"Where the hell you been at, girl?" Maria's friend asked heatedly.

"We went to the store after D.J. showed me his rims he bought today," she replied.

"Yeah, that probably ain't the only thing he showed you," Kev blurted under his breath.

I'm sure everybody knew what the deal was. They probably didn't know exactly what happened, but they figured something had gone down. The smile I had on my face was so big, I'm sure any one of them could sense the guilt.

"Take this brew, nigga," Dre said. "Didn't you say you had to talk to us about some shit, dog?" he asked.

"Yeah, but not in front of everybody," I answered.

I guess Maria and her friends got the point because they moved from our table to the edge of the pool so they could drench their feet.

"Yo, that chick Maria just gave me the best brain I've had in a minute, maybe even ever," I said energetically.

"Stop lying, nigga, I don't believe you," Kev said.

"I swear to God, right in the Caddie, dog," I contested. "I bullshit you not!"

"Fuck all that, D.J.," Fat Chris said. "What is so important that you had to chase the chicks away to tell us?"

"Oh yeah," I said. "Shit is starting to get a little crazy out here."

"What you mean, dog?" Dre asked.

"Word on the street is that niggas have noticed that we've been spending hella cash lately."

"So the fuck what?" he said. "I wish somebody would try to fuck with any one of us. I'll lay a nigga down in a second," Dre said boastfully.

"It's not just about that, though, dog," I replied. "If the word is out, the jakes might have caught wind of shit, too."

"Fuck the cops," said Fat Chris.

"Yeah, that's easy for you to say, nigga," Kev complained. "I'm about to go into the NFL. I can't afford to get caught up in this shit."

"Exactly, that's why I'm not taking any more jewelry to my connection," I said. "I made one last drop yesterday, so this last money I have for y'all niggas is it. I'm done with this shit," I said sternly.

"How much?" Joey asked.

"Six grand each," I replied.

"Hold up, dog," Fat Chris shouted loudly. "I know that last drop wasn't worth no thirty thousand dollars. How the fuck are you giving us six grand each?"

"I figured that this shit was going to end sometime, so I started putting some of the money away."

"Nah, fuck that, D.J., you been holding out on niggas," alleged Chris.

"Don't fuckin' come at me like that, dog," I shouted violently. "I've been giving y'all thousands every week. That's what's wrong with niggas today! Everybody always gotta have more money, more jewels, more cars, and more of all that other material bullshit that means nothing. Society needs to get off that dumb shit."

"Hold up, you just went and bought some new rims for your Cadillac with money that we made from robbing niggas," Dre uttered. "Don't act like you're better than anybody else."

Dre was right. Maybe I wasn't any better. I was caught up in the same mind-set. I just didn't have the guts to admit it to myself. I guess that Saturday just happened to be my day of reckoning.

"We don't have a fuckin' college degree, dog," Fat Chris roared. "Ain't no corporate job waiting for us, sellout."

"Look, the shit is over," I said. "Come to my car and get your fuckin' money and don't fool with me since I'm a muthafuckin' sellout."

"Y'all niggas need to just chill," cried Kev.

"Fuck this shit," I shouted. "I'm leaving in a few weeks anyway! Come get your money out my car. I'm done with y'all niggas."

"You on some real bitch shit right now, D.J.," Dre said calmly as the argument came to a close.

We all walked over to my car in complete silence. I pulled the safe from my trunk and gave each of them what I said I would—six grand. Fat Chris and Dre snatched their cash and hustled back over to the pool. Kev and Joey stayed by the car to try to calm the situation. I didn't really feel like talking, so I cut the conversation very short.

"I will holla at y'all niggas later," I said. "I gotta go meet up with Tara anyway."

"Hit me up later on," Kev replied. "We probably gonna come through."

"Nah, don't worry about it. I'm gonna be with my girl. I'll see y'all another time," I returned.

We slapped hands and I got in the car so I could leave. This great day had quickly taken a turn for the worse. I looked down at my watch and saw that it was just before six thirty. I told Tara that I was going to be at her house at one o'clock, and on top of that, I hadn't called her all day.

I knew that as soon as I saw her, I'd be arguing with her for a couple hours, too. I thought about not even going to her house, but that was probably the worst decision I could make.

I turned the music on full blast and kept cruising. *HAPPY FUCKIN' BIRTHDAY to me,* I said to myself.

I didn't even know where I was going at that point. I just kept driving and driving.

TEN

pulled into Tara's parents' driveway a few minutes past two in the morning. I had spent the majority of my day thinking about the critical situation that I had found myself in. I just had to let things cool down for a while. Though I was glad that I had finally put an end to it all, I was still worried about Dre and the rest of the League. Quite frankly, this was best for all of us, so I was comfortable with my decision.

Tara had already opened the door and was standing in the breezeway with her hands glued to her hips before I stepped out of the car. She must have heard me creep into the driveway.

Here we go, I thought.

I really didn't feel like arguing, but I knew that this disagreement was inevitable. I took it head-on.

"What the fuck, D.J.?" she shouted.

"Shhhh! It's two o'clock in the morning and your parents are sleeping," I said calmly.

"My parents aren't even fuckin' here, dumb-ass. They went to Atlantic City for the weekend so we could have some privacy!" she screamed.

"Babe, I'm so sorry," I pleaded.

"You ain't fuckin' sorry, D.J.," she said. "You did exactly what you wanted to do on your birthday. You ran around with those stupid-ass friends of yours!"

"It wasn't even like that," I explained.

"Don't give me that bullshit," she screamed. "I already told your mom what's going on with you and them, too."

"What are you talking about?"

"I'm not fuckin' stupid," she said. "I know where y'all been getting all that money."

Apparently, she had known how we had been cashing in all along. As much as I tried to keep it away from her, I should have known that she'd figure it out sooner or later. There were times when she asked me what I had in the black book bag, but I never suspected that she'd ever opened it. She usually didn't bother my personal belongings. I guess this time she couldn't resist.

"It's a damn shame that you neglected me to go hang out with a bunch of niggas that don't give a fuck about you," said Tara.

"C'mon with that bullshit," I replied.

"If they did, you wouldn't be the one in the middle of this shit now," she countered.

"I ended it all today, Tara. I told all them niggas that I was done."

"You're gonna end up getting hurt or going to fuckin' jail over some dumb shit," she whimpered. "You have your whole life ahead of you, D.J."

"I know, Tara, I know," I said. "Come here."

I hugged her tightly as she cried out all of her tears. My shirt felt like it had just come out of a wash machine when she finished. I hated it when she cried, especially when I was responsible for her pain. We went upstairs to get comfortable and I began giving her a back massage so she could relax.

"Don't go to sleep," I said. "I have something to tell you."

"D.J., I had enough drama for one night. Just tell me tomorrow, babe, please."

"It can't want until tomorrow because that's when we leave," I explained.

"Where are we going?" she asked.

"I booked us a trip to Vegas so we can get away for a few days," I whispered.

She sat up quickly. Tara loved to gamble.

"What about my job, D.J.?" she replied. "I can't miss work."

"I already took care of it. You have the whole week off," I said.

Her feelings were still hurt, but she had no choice but to smile. I knew she was excited.

"Are we staying at the Bellagio?"

"You know it," I said boldly.

All she ever talked about was going to the water show, so I couldn't go wrong with that choice. She hugged me so tightly that she damn near stopped me from breathing. I immediately felt a mass of guilt come over me because of what I had done in the car earlier.

"Get some sleep, babe, I know you're tired," I said. "Our plane leaves the airport at ten fifty in the morning, plus we have to get up early to pack."

"I love you, D.J.," she said.

"I love you more," I replied.

I gave her a kiss and watched as she fell into a deep sleep. Sleeping wasn't an option for me that night. I was too busy reflecting on everything that had happened since graduation. I knew that I needed to straighten up, but I continued acting as if I had everything under control.

I was glad to get the hell out of the city, though. Tara and I needed to be able to just enjoy each other for once.

ELEVEN

Our trip felt like it had ended as soon as it began. Though it breezed by quickly, Tara and I surely had a time to remember. The instant we got back to Harrisburg, Tara insisted that we go to a jewelry store to hunt down a bracelet that she'd seen in Vegas. I decided to take her to see Tony because I knew if he didn't have it, he would know someone that did or he'd just make it himself.

It was Friday afternoon so I was sure that the mall would be pretty busy. It took me about twenty minutes just to find a parking spot. After I finally tracked one down, we headed straight for the District. Tony was always excited to see me because my presence meant money.

"Wussup, D.J., you got something for me today?" Tony asked.

"Nah, not today, boss . . . just doing a little shopping for the lady," I said. "Babe, go ahead and look around. I'm going to holla at Tony for a few."

"Well, you are too late this week anyway," he replied.

"What do you mean, too late?" I asked.

"Two of your friends came in yesterday and made this week's drop," he responded. "They said you told them to drop it off and get the cash because you'd be out of town for a few days."

"Fuck no! I didn't tell them to bring you shit," I said angrily. "They didn't even know that you were the one I was dealing with!"

"Well, they know now," he said quickly.

As I stood listening to Tony, I didn't just become angry, I was furious. I couldn't believe they went behind my back after I shut things down. Tara's bracelet had to wait. It was time to go . . . immediately.

"How much cash did you give them?" I asked.

"Seventy-five hundred," said Tony. "It was some pretty good stuff, too! I should make a nice profit!"

"Look, don't fuckin' give them any more money and don't accept any more jewelry. This operation is fuckin' over," I growled.

"Relax, bro, business is business . . . nothing personal," he said spitefully.

"Fuck this shit, let's go, Tara," I shouted.

"D.J., I didn't even get to—" she pleaded.

"Let's go, *now*," I screamed loudly.

I was so upset that I could not remember where I had parked. Tara kept asking what was wrong, but I stayed silent as we tracked down the car and got moving.

Three minutes after we left the mall, my cell phone rang and I had hoped that it would be one of my boys. I was in for a big surprise.

"Hello."

"D.J., what the hell is wrong with you?"

"What now, Mom, what's the problem?" I asked.

"Don't play with me, goddammit," she countered. "I just got off the phone with Detective Kinard from downtown."

"What's that got to do with me?" I asked.

"Don't act like you don't know, D.J.," she rumbled. "He said the department has caught wind of what you and your friends have been up to."

My heart began racing uncontrollably.

"They are trying to build a case against you guys as we speak," she cried. "The only reason I know is because Kinard is my friend and he remembered your name from your days playing football. You better stop whatever you're into," she screamed. "You're gonna ruin your damn life! I taught you better than this!"

"I'm done with it already," I replied. "I have been out of town, Mom, and you know that."

"If I get another call from Kinard, you will be going to talk to him personally and that's final," she ordered.

I tried to respond, but she promptly hung up the phone in my face. Even though I didn't want to, I had to call my friends to let them know what had just happened. I dialed Dre because I figured that he and Fat Chris were the only ones who would have gone to see Tony behind my back. I was right.

"What's good, my nigga?" he answered.

"Ain't nothing fuckin' good, Dre," I shouted. "Why the fuck would you go to the District behind my back like that?"

"You said you were done," he replied. "The party don't stop because you say it does. I'm feeding my damn family, nigga."

"You won't be feeding them for too long because you can't do shit from a jail cell," I uttered. "A detective called my crib and they know what's going down. I tried to tell y'all niggas to chill with all that shit!"

"I don't give a fuck," he returned.

"That's why I'm not fuckin' with none of y'all niggas anymore," I said. "If y'all get caught, don't put my name in nothing."

"You the only one that would probably snitch, college boy," he replied. "And you know snitches get stitches around here."

"Are you threatening me, dog?" I shouted. "Just keep my name out of your mouth. Y'all niggas don't even exist to me."

"I'm not trying to hear this bullshit," Dre replied. "I'll holla at you later. You must be on your period or some shit, nigga. You are turning into a real female."

"Karma is a bitch, dog," I said. "It's gonna get your ass sooner or later."

I hung up before Dre could respond. I called Kev to let him know what was going on because I knew that he had a lot to lose, just like I did. He decided that he was finished, too, which I was happy to hear. I had to clear my head, so Tara and I headed back to her house. I was hoping that her parents weren't there. Luckily, they were just leaving as we pulled up.

"Hey, D.J.," Tara's mom said excitedly.

"Hey, Mrs. Lewis, Mr. Lewis, how is everything?"

"Good, did you guys have fun?" Mr. Lewis asked.

"Yes, Dad, we're just tired," Tara responded. "We will see y'all when you get back."

"Okay, honey, we want to hear about the trip, so don't leave," said Mrs. Lewis.

I was glad that Tara bailed us out. I was in no mood to be chatting with parents, not even my own. We went straight to Tara's room, where I promptly fell to the middle of the floor. As always, she was there to pick me up.

"Turn your phone off, D.J.," she said as she knelt down beside me. "Just try to get some rest, please."

"I can't take this shit anymore," I returned. "I can't wait until I leave this place. Everybody around me is on bullshit!"

"Even me, babe?" she asked.

"Of course not . . . you are the only one in my life that isn't crazy," I replied.

Honestly, she was the only one that I could confide in at that point. I didn't feel like I had anyone else. My actions were finally catching up with me. I didn't think things could get any worse.

Thank God I had Tara.

TWELVE

I didn't wake up the next day until late in the afternoon. When I opened my eyes, I noticed that Tara wasn't around. I shuffled to my feet so I could use the bathroom. As I passed the mirror, I stared for about thirty seconds, trying to figure out who or what I was looking at. Yes, it was me, but I did not like the person that I had my eyes on. When she walked in, I was still peering at my own reflection.

"What are you doing, D.J.?" asked Tara.

"Nothing, why?" I replied.

"Well, good morning to you, too. Your mom called me a few times, she wants you to come home."

"For what?" I asked.

"D.J., I don't know, I'm just the messenger."

I already knew what it was about. She wanted to have a heart-to-heart conversation with me. Anytime she was disappointed in me, she'd sit me down and make me feel like I was the worst person in the world. She wouldn't yell or scream at all. She was always calm and spoke in a voice that was very relaxed and nonthreatening. Her words still cut like a sword, though. I guess mothers always know how to get to their children. I left Tara's house quickly so I could prepare myself before I arrived home to hear the sermon.

"Mommy," I shouted as I walked in the front door.

"Come in the kitchen, son," she responded. "Do you want me to make you some lunch?"

"Nah, I'm not in the eating mood right now," I said.

"Well, come sit your ass down anyway," she replied. "I don't wanna fight with you, honey, but you need to be put in your place and guess who is going to do it."

"Let me guess? You, Mom," I mumbled.

"You're so smart," she said. "That is why I am puzzled how a kid so smart manages to make decisions that are so damn dumb."

"I know, Mom," I said. "You're absolutely right."

"I know I'm right, D.J.," she replied. "You need to remember that when I'm not watching you, God is. He expects more from you. *I* expect more from you."

"I know you are disappointed in me and I'm sorry," I said remorsefully. "I only have a few weeks left before I leave and I will be walking the straight and narrow every step I take."

"You took the words right out of my mouth, son," she answered. "I expect you will do exactly that."

"I promise you I will," I said as I stared at the floor.

She spent the next forty-five minutes making me feel guilty about not setting the right example for my little brothers, upon other things. She was right about everything that she said so there was no room for argument. Our conversation ended with her usual phrase alluding to the fact that she is still the boss. When she uttered those words, she really meant that her lecture was over and I could leave.

I left the kitchen feeling much better than I had before I entered. My comfort would be interrupted again when my cell phone rang. I hadn't heard from Bum in a while so I was happy that he was calling. Ever since we began cashing in, he didn't hang around us anymore because he was angry that I hadn't included him in our scheme. He was a really cool cat who I'd known from junior high, but I just didn't know if I could trust him.

"What's good, nigga?" I answered eagerly. "Why you been hiding from us, dog?"

"Some shit went down," he replied. "I haven't been hiding. I just got lost for a little while. I wasn't gonna stand around and watch y'all enjoy all that money while I'm starving."

"It wasn't even like that," I said. "You could have got down with us, but I didn't think you were with it, though."

"Whatever, y'all niggas played me," he returned. "That's not why I called you, though. The reason I called is because Fat Chris is in the hospital."

"Why, what happened?" I asked.

"Some nigga stabbed him in the stomach a couple times. He's in critical condition," he added.

"Fuck, what hospital?" I asked.

"The one downtown," he said. "We're already down here in the parking lot right now."

"I'm walking out the door," I replied as I hung up the phone.

I must have made it to the hospital in ten minutes. It was usually a twenty- or thirty-minute drive. When I arrived, everybody was sitting in the waiting room not saying a word. Kev was the first to break the eerie silence.

"Wussup, dog, he gonna be okay we think," he said despondently.

"What the hell happened?" I asked.

"Somebody ran up on him in the 'hood and tried to rob him. You know Chris ain't giving up shit, so they poked him up."

"How many times did they stab him?"

"Eight times," he replied.

"Damn, this shit is getting too crazy," I returned. "But what goes around comes around, though. I keep trying to tell niggas that, but y'all won't listen."

"We ain't trying to hear your preaching," said Dre. "My nigga is lying in there sliced up. Go somewhere else with that bullshit," he added.

"Keep talking reckless, Dre," I uttered. "Your mouth is gonna get you in trouble."

"Y'all niggas need to shut the fuck up," Joey said. "We're all brothers in here. Stop arguing and start thinking about how we gonna find these niggas that did this!"

"Don't worry about that. I'm gonna take care of it," said Dre. "You know every nigga in here ain't down to ride no more."

"Dead this shit. . . . Here comes the doctor," Bum said.

Everybody stood up to hear what he had to say. I was bracing myself for bad news because my cousin had gotten stabbed in the gut a while back and died as a result of his wounds.

"Hello, gentlemen," the doctor said. "Surgery went well. Other than the eighty-six stitches holding him together, he's doing all right."

"Thank God," I whispered.

"It's no use for you guys to stay at this point as he needs to get rest. Besides, he won't be seeing visitors until at least the day after tomorrow."

That was all I needed to hear. Even though it was unfortunate that he had gotten stabbed, I still felt the same way about things. I wasn't going to get wrapped up in any more mishaps. I was sure that they were going to try to do some damage to the dudes that stabbed Fat Chris. I didn't want any part of it. I had enough on my conscience already.

"I'm gonna holla at y'all later," I said. "I have a lot of shit going on right now."

"A'ight, dog, I'll get at you," Kev replied. "I'll keep you posted."

"Whatever y'all do, be safe," I said as I marched off.

I slapped hands with everybody except Dre before I walked out of the automatic doors. The ironic thing about it was that he and I had known one another since we were twelve years old. We were tight before the League was even created. That's what made the situation so bad.

I called Tara and told her everything that had happened. Anything could make her cry, so she broke down just as I thought she would. She met me at my house looking like a hurricane had hit her. My mom thought that I had done something to hurt her again. I did not want to tell her what had really happened, but Tara couldn't keep her mouth shut.

Two heart-to-heart conversations in one day is one too many, I said to myself as I listened to them chatting.

To my dismay, my mom called me to the kitchen again. But this time I was talking and she was listening.

THIRTEEN

I woke up in a cold sweat in the early hours of Sunday morning. I was a little disturbed because Chris died at the hospital in a dream that I had. Knowing that I would not be able to go back to sleep, I trudged downstairs to watch TV so I wouldn't wake Tara. Minutes later, she showed up anyway.

"What are you doing, D.J.?"

"Nothing, I couldn't sleep," I replied.

"Are you okay?"

"Yes, babe, I just had a bad dream," I said. "Fat Chris

died in the hospital and everybody was going crazy. It was terrible."

"Chris is gonna be fine, D.J."

"I know. Go back to sleep. I'll be okay," I whispered.

"You sure?" she asked.

"I'm positive."

She went back upstairs and left me to my thoughts. For some reason, I just wanted to be alone. I slept on and off until about nine thirty in the morning. Tara had promised to go to church with her parents, so she came downstairs to say good-bye as soon as I awoke.

"I'm leaving, babe, what are you gonna do today?"

"I don't know, probably just hit the gym and chill out."

"Call me later then," she replied.

"Wait, Tara can I ask you a question?"

"Yeah, what is it, babe?"

"Why do you think people are so worried about having so much money and buying all kind of shit that is just for show?" I asked.

"I don't know, D.J." she said. "I think society has conditioned us into believing that what is on the outside is what counts."

"Society is fucking all of us up," I said. "That's why

the richer get richer, the poorer get poorer, and the middle class stays stuck in between."

"Yep, just the way rich people like it," she returned.

"Rich people ain't the only problem," I said. "Niggas just need to wake up and start realizing that these money-hungry lifestyles are only going to lead to a dead end."

"You're right, baby."

"Maybe I need to get a record deal and rap about how stupid niggas are that spend all of their cash on cars, strip clubs, and jewelry," I added. "Then maybe things would change."

"You've been acting just like those idiots lately. How about you take a look in the mirror and make some changes to yourself first. Plus, that wouldn't work anyway," Tara continued. "These music companies only give chances to black people that rap about all that nonsense, while rock bands get record deals and shoot videos in ripped-up jeans and T-shirts."

She was absolutely right. We went on discussing how screwed up America was for about ten minutes and then she left. We both agreed that the only way that our culture would change is if the people that lead it stop steering it in the wrong direction. I didn't help the cause by thrusting my boys and me into an illegal operation that afforded us a little extra money.

It was now late afternoon and I knew I couldn't sit around the house all day. I decided to take my little brother's pit bull to the park. I went out to the backyard to snatch him up. Korey came through the gate as I was putting Kilo on the leash.

"Where you going with my dog, D.J.?" he asked.

"Just to the park for a little bit," I said.

"Don't let him off the leash. You know I'm the only person he listens to. He got a little too much power for you."

"Whatever, I'm the one who trained him," I returned. "I got this."

"I'm taking my driver's test tomorrow," said Korey.

"You can't drive worth shit," I uttered. "You probably gonna fail."

"Why are you trying to jinx me like that? If I pass, can I take the Caddie for a spin tomorrow?"

"We'll see," I replied. "Just pass the test first, then holla at me."

This might sound cruel, but I was hoping that he wouldn't pass. I had just put new rims on my ride not too long ago and I didn't want to risk getting them ruined by a rookie driver. I remembered how it was to be at that age, though, so if he did pass, I was going to let him go for a little spin as long as I was in the passenger seat.

◆

The next day, I was wishing that I hadn't opened my mouth. Korey burst in the door at about four o'clock screaming for me. I knew this meant that he had passed his driver's test, so I snatched my keys off the dresser and went downstairs.

"Chill out or I'm not letting you drive," I said. "Don't be all hype because if you wreck my shit, I'm gonna wreck you."

"Watch your mouth, D.J.! You're grown, but don't think you can curse in front of me. You aren't around those hoodlums you hang with."

"My bad, Mom," I replied. "I just want to make sure that your son knows that if he puts one scratch on my car, I'm gonna have to destroy him."

"I'll be careful, D.J.," said Korey. "I promise!"

Before we left, I made him clean my entire car. I was going to let him drive, but not without working him first.

As we pulled off, his smile reminded me of how I felt the first time I got behind the wheel as a young dude.

"Can we stop over Seth's house so I can show off?"

"Nah, go toward the city. I wanna stop by Kev's crib," I said.

I had to laugh as we got moving because he was leaned back in the seat like he was me. He knew that you couldn't push the Cadillac posted too close to the wheel. We stopped off at Double D's so I could get a six-pack to sip while he escorted me around town. The weather was perfect, my car was immaculate, and I had an ice-cold brew in my lap. Those types of days when everything was ideal were very rare that summer.

Korey kept begging me to allow him to pass by his friend's house. We had already been in the streets for hours, but I decided to let him do his thing. We stopped by Seth's house before I let him parade through the neighborhood where he spent most of his time.

You could tell that this was one of his happiest moments. Nobody could knock his hustle that day, not even me. He was happy . . . so I was happy, too.

FOURTEEN

The day was drawing to a close, so I finally told Korey to head back to the crib. We had been in the streets all day. I ended up filling up my tank twice, which pissed me off because gas prices were ridiculous. It was getting dark, so I told Korey to turn on the lights. You could tell he was a rookie.

"Slow down, li'l nigga," I said. "Stop getting so close to people. If they slam on their brakes and you hit them, the cops gonna say it's your fault."

"My bad, D.J."

"It's all good," I replied. "See what I mean. You got fools like this that stop and the light barely even turned yellow," I said as he slammed on the brakes.

"I saw him, though," he returned. "I'm not gonna wreck."

We were sitting at the red light for about thirty seconds when our situation took an extraordinary turn. Out of the corner of my eye, I noticed an SUV pull behind us on the driver's side. Someone hopped out and ran up to Korey's window. It felt like everything happened in a split second.

"Get out the fuckin' car before I put your brains on the steering wheel, nigga!"

"What the *fuck*!" I shouted.

This cat had his gun to the side of Korey's head. I knew my brother wasn't built for this type of situation so I immediately tried to take control. He was glaring over at me with a look of terror on his face that I will never forget. He was just frozen.

"Hold up, nigga, this is my car," I said.

"I don't give a fuck! Both of y'all better get the fuck out of the car before somebody gets blasted!"

My mind was going crazy. I didn't care what happened to me, Korey was the one I was worried about. The dude mashed the gun up against Korey's temple as the light turned green and I could tell he was serious so I had to think quickly.

"Step on the gas," I whispered low enough that only Korey could hear me. "Nowww!" I shouted.

I know I told him to step on it, but he was so terrified that he put the pedal to the floor. The sound of burnt rubber on pavement could be heard from blocks away. I grabbed the steering wheel as we sped off, but our trouble was far from over.

Bang . . . bang . . . bang, bang, bang!

I turned around and noticed that the rear window of my car was completely shattered. My adrenaline was pumping so hard, I didn't even know that I was hit. I glanced over at Korey and saw that his T-shirt was soaked with blood. Bullets from the gun had pierced both of us.

"Oh shit, stop the car!"

"Ahhhhhhhh . . . my back, D.J.!" he screamed.

He eased on the brakes. I guided the steering wheel toward the curb and hopped out of the car while it was still coasting forward. I didn't care that I was shot. I had to tend to my little brother. Once Korey saw that he was bleeding so badly, he began to panic.

"He really . . . he shot me, D.J.," he said as if he was losing his breath. "I'm gonna die."

"Shit, get up out the car so I can lay you in the back."

I snatched him out of the driver's side and laid him down in the backseat. There was so much blood around that it started to make me sick. I jumped in the driver's seat and sped off. I hit the highway and darted to the hospital as quickly as I could. I kept telling Korey to stay with me, but I was the one getting faint. I drove up on the sidewalk at the entrance of the emergency room and lugged Korey through the glass doors after I yanked him out of the car.

"I need a fuckin' doctor, *now*. My brother just got shot," I hollered.

"Calm down, sir, sit him down right here."

"I'm not fuckin' calming down, get me a doctor!"

Another nurse ran from the back with a stretcher. We hoisted Korey onto it and she and two others rushed him down the hallway. The room was filled with people, but for some reason it seemed like I was all alone. An old lady beside me told me that I was bleeding from my shoulder. I felt the sting, but nothing mattered except Korey at that point. I sat down in one of the chairs and covered my face with my bloody hands. My mind was gone. I didn't know what the hell to do. I pulled out my cell phone and called Tara.

"Hello?"

"Baby, come to the hospital downtown right now. Me and my little brother both got shot!"

"No, D.J., oh my God, nooooo," she cried. "I'm coming right now!"

"Call my mom!"

Another nurse came out and told me that I had to go back and get my shoulder treated. The more I sat in the waiting room, the more it began to hurt, but all I was worried about was my brother.

"I'm good, ma'am. Can you just tell me how Korey is doing?"

"As soon as I know something, you will know something," she said. "In the meantime, I am taking you back to treat your wound. It's not an option, mister. You don't have a choice. Get up now and let's go," she commanded.

Reluctantly, I slowly stood up and followed her back to the triage room. She told me that it looked as if the bullet went all the way through, but that I may need stitches. She then escorted me to another room where a doctor was waiting to see me.

"You are very lucky, son," he said. "A few inches to the right and that bullet could have been life-threatening."

I sat silently as he checked me out. He called the nurse

back in and told her that I would need a few stitches, so she began preparing the room.

"We have to numb you up, son, this may hurt a bit," he said as he inserted a large needle into the back of my left shoulder.

"Just get it over with," I replied. "I need to see how my brother is."

It took him about twenty minutes to finish stitching me up. Even though I only needed a few stitches, he wanted to make sure that the wound was dressed correctly. The burning sensation continued, but it felt better after they mobilized my left arm with a sling. They had me sitting in there for at least two hours. I told both of them that I felt fine just so I could hurry back to see what Korey's status was. When I walked back out to the waiting room, Dre and Tara were speaking to a nurse behind the crowded reception desk. As soon as she caught eye contact with me, she started crying and ran up to hug me.

"Are you okay, baby? My heart can't take this anymore!"

"I'm fine. What did they say about my brother?" I asked.

"He gonna be all right," said Dre. "He got hit three times—two in his upper back and one slightly grazed his neck. How you feeling?" he asked.

"I'm fine, dog . . . this nigga fuckin' shot my little brother."

"Do you know who it was?"

"Not really, but he did look familiar," I replied. "The only thing I remember is that he had a tattoo on his right hand that said 'M.O.B.' I saw it when he had his gun to Korey's head."

"Oh shit, what did the letters look like?"

"They were in cursive and it looked like blood or something was dripping off of them," I answered.

"That's one of them niggas that we beat down at the Firefly the day of your graduation. I remember that tattoo like it was yesterday because I snatched his watch off his wrist. I'm gonna kill both them muthafuckas!"

"Dre, ain't gonna be no killing. Can you just leave my boyfriend alone? You already got him into enough shit. Now his little brother is dragged in it, too," Tara cried.

I was shocked because Dre didn't even say anything. I couldn't get Tara to stop crying, so I took her outside to calm her down a little. Minutes later, Dre came out and told me that one of the nurses was looking for me, so I hurried back inside.

"I'm D.J., ma'am. I'm Korey's older brother."

"He is going to be just fine," she said.

"Did they get the bullets out of his back?" I asked.

"Yes, they did, but he will be on a liquid diet for at least three days," she replied. "He is also going to have to stay for a while."

"Well, can I go check on him?"

"I know you want to, but he has been through a lot in the past couple hours, so the doctor doesn't want anyone bothering him tonight. He needs to rest."

"He's only seventeen years old," I said. "I know he needs me right now."

"I'm sure, honey, but he took it like a man and seeing him is not possible right at this moment. He's a real tough kid, so don't be worried. You should go home and get some rest yourself," she suggested. "After all, you were shot, too."

"Their mother is on her way, so we are going to stay and wait," said Tara.

"Well, that's a good idea. Make yourselves at home. If you need anything, just holler."

"Thank you, ma'am," I whispered.

Tara hustled over to the vending machine to grab a drink for me. When she sat down, I laid my head in her lap and watched every person who paced through the door. I knew that sooner or later, my mom would be striding in. I did not know what I was going to say to her. I fell asleep for a few minutes, only to be awakened by a familiar voice.

"Wake up, son," she said. "Are you okay?"

"Yes, Mom, we both are fine," I replied as I regained consciousness.

"You have some explaining to do."

As my vision began to clear, I noticed that someone was standing behind her. First I thought it was Dre, but when I sat up, I was in for a rude awakening.

I had never seen this man before, but somehow I knew it was a cop just from his demeanor. Plus, he had a .357 Magnum attached to his hip, which was a dead giveaway.

It wasn't just some random officer, though. It was Detective Kinard.

FIFTEEN

It was bothering me that my mom hadn't acted too worried when she arrived at the hospital. She was the type of person who went crazy if her children were harmed in any way.

Apparently, Tara had already spoken to her several times on the phone when I was getting stitched up. She had assured her that everything was okay, so as a result my mom began thinking about what she was going to do next. That was probably why she had called Detective Kinard before she rushed to the hospital. I didn't know if I was prepared for the onslaught of questions that followed.

"Your brother just got two bullets removed from his back with your name on them," said Detective Kinard. "Are you ready to talk now?"

"What do you mean, 'with my name on them'?" I asked. "Are you saying that this is my fault?"

"Are you saying that it's not?"

I really did not know how to respond to his question. In a way, I guess I was somewhat responsible because Korey was with me. The streets don't follow rules, so anybody can end up being a victim. It took that day to make me realize that.

"With all due respect, sir, don't suggest that I meant for this to happen."

"Son, I know you didn't mean for it to happen. The question is . . . what are you going to do now?"

"What do you wanna know?" I asked.

"I want to know it all," he replied.

There was no way that I was going to give up any names involved nor give any details about what we had been into that summer. I could tell that's what he wanted to hear; he was less worried about the shooting. He wanted to know about the money scheme. I gave him a brief description of the perpetrator who'd shot my brother and shut my mouth.

"Do you think I'm a damn fool, D.J.?" rumbled Detective Kinard. "I get the feeling that you assume I was born yesterday, son."

"Sir, he tried to carjack us. He put his gun to my little brother's head and told both of us to get out the car."

"So the incident was a botched attempt to steal your vehicle?" he asked.

"I don't know, I guess."

"It seems very coincidental that he chose your car out of the many he could have picked, don't you think?"

"Look, sir . . . I just put new rims on my car. I wasn't letting him drive away with my vehicle."

"I guess those rims were worth more than your brother's life, huh?" he asked.

"What type of question is that?" I replied angrily. "You keep digging for something and there is nothing else I have to give."

"You better hope there isn't because if there is, I am definitely going to get to the bottom of it. Trust me," he shouted. "I have one last question for you."

"Okay?"

"What is your relationship with Andre Banks?"

When he asked me that question, I discreetly glanced behind me to see if Dre was still at the hospital. He was sitting a few rows back sound asleep, but Kinard had no idea that it was actually him.

"We have been friends since we were kids, why do you ask?" I said.

"I just have a few questions for him, so if you do happen to see him, give him this card so he can give me a call. It's in his best interest to get in contact with me as soon as possible."

"I will," I replied.

"Is there anything else you think I should know?"

"No, sir, I told you everything."

"I hear that you are leaving for the army in a few weeks. I'd stay off the streets if I were you," he uttered. "I don't know why you hang out in town anyway. You live in a white-picket-fence neighborhood, maybe that's where you should stay."

"A lot more bad things happen in the 'burbs than in the city, the cops just don't know or ignore it," I replied.

"Well, I have eyes everywhere and if I get any negative reporting about you or anyone you associate with, I am going to make it my personal business to crush all of you."

During most of our conversation, I was looking at the ground, but his last comment made me look him directly in his face.

"Are we clear?" he asked.

"Crystal," I replied.

He shook his head and shuffled across the waiting room to where Tara and my mom were seated. Tara came over and sat beside me with a troubled look on her face.

"What was all that about, D.J.?"

"Nothing, babe, he was asking me questions about the shooting and Dre," I said. "I ain't have shit to tell him, though."

"Promise me something, D.J.," she said.

"What?"

"Don't go looking for the guy that did this. Let the law take care of it, D.J. You have too much to lose."

"Everybody in the world got shit to lose, not just me," I replied.

"That is true. I was talking to your mom and some things are about to change, though."

"Like what?"

"She'll have to be the one to tell you," she replied. "She is sitting in a hospital with two of her three sons shot and I am not gonna be any more of a thorn in her side."

I had no idea how to take what Tara had just said to me. I did know that my mom was hurting very badly at this point. I couldn't cause her any more pain, so I decided to let things blow over for a while. I watched as she and Detective Kinard finished talking to the nurses. I was sure it was good news because my mom smiled a few times.

As they headed to the door, she walked past me without even saying good-bye. She just gave me a peculiar look that I could not decipher. I was yearning to know what Tara was talking about, but for now I wasn't going anywhere until my little brother was ready to go home. I didn't care how many days he would have to stay.

The hospital would be where I spent both my days and my nights until Korey was well enough to leave.

SIXTEEN

Thursday morning was a joyous day—Korey was finally discharged. Family and friends had been in and out of the hospital since the day of the shooting, but I was the only one who hadn't left once. It felt like I had the same clothing on for two weeks. As we prepared to leave the hospital, I could tell that his spirits were much better. I was happy because when we made it outside, I noticed that the back window was already fixed in my car. My uncle Mike could repair anything or knew somebody who could, so I was sure he had something to do with it getting fixed.

"Can I drive home, D.J.?" asked Korey.

"You still wanna drive after all the shit we have been through?"

"Yeah, why not?" he replied.

"You can barely move, let alone drive. Plus, the last time you drove, we had bullets flying at us."

"Are we gonna go after him?" he asked.

"We aren't doing shit! You are gonna relax for the next couple of weeks so you can heal up," I followed. "Don't worry about none of that revenge bullshit. Enough bad things have happened in the last couple weeks, anyway, and Mommy is already worried to death."

"Yeah, I know," said Korey.

"Exactly, so that means keep your ass out of the streets."

"What makes you think that you should be in the 'hood?" said Korey. "Ain't no such thing as a thug with a college degree."

"Being a thug is overrated, Korey. I ain't no thug and I don't ever want to be one," I returned. "Bullets don't discriminate, though. They kill everybody the same, whether you from South Philly or Beverly Hills. You can find real niggas in every city or town, no matter where you at," I added. "Just because a nigga ain't from the 'hood doesn't mean he won't pull a trigger. Look at the shit that Dre does."

It was too bad that he had to learn what I was explaining to him the hard way. After all, it was my fault. I was speaking the truth, though. Since hip-hop made being a thug cool, it seemed like pop culture just followed suit. The last thing on my mind was seeking retribution. I had too many other things to worry about, my life especially. I was leaving for training in a few weeks and I knew I had a lot of loose ends to tie up. There was no way I was going to allow my brother or me to end up a statistic.

As we got closer to our house, I began to wonder how my mom was going to react when we got home. I knew she was going to be happy that we both were okay, but for the last few days at the hospital she was a bit distant. Maybe it was because two of her sons just got shot, but something just didn't seem right.

We burst through the door and were greeted by the sweet smell of eggs and smoked bacon.

"My babies are home," she said eagerly.

"What's up, Mom? It feels good to come home to a home-cooked meal. That hospital food was gross," Korey said.

"Both of y'all go wash your hands so you can eat."

"I will eat later. I'm going to go clean my car out. It's a mess," I replied.

"Well, you make sure you come right back here. We need to talk," she said firmly.

"I hear you, Mom," I returned.

I walked out to the garage to grab all of my cleaning supplies. My car still had spots of dried-up blood all over the seats. I told Korey to hurry up and make himself useful if possible. After all, he was the one who'd bled all over the place.

"Korey, you ain't going nowhere. Your butt is mine for now. You need to get your stuff together anyway."

"What stuff, Mom?"

"Everything," she uttered.

I walked out of the door while they were going back and forth. She seemed like she was in good spirits, so that eased my stress level, considering what I had been through the last few days.

I must have scrubbed my leather down for at least an hour and a half. The smell of Clorox was so strong that it began making me queasy as I drove back from the car wash. It felt as if I had just sprayed a liter of disinfectant up my nose.

I pulled into the driveway and sat in silence for a few minutes. I had to figure out what I was going to do to get things back under control. My mom must have been waiting on her heels for me to return because she hustled outside and jumped into my car as soon as she spotted me.

"It smells like a damn gallon of Clorox in here. Did you use the whole bottle, son?"

"Yes, Mom, I had to make sure everything was clean," I replied. "Before you say anything, I just wanted to say that I'm sorry for putting Korey in that situation."

"Look, don't go there, D.J.," she said. "I know you didn't mean for any of this to happen, but when you don't follow God's path, the devil always intervenes."

"When I saw Korey bleeding like that, I felt like my world was crumbling," I said in a chalky voice.

"I can imagine," she replied. "That's why you have to think before you act. You know what goes around comes around. I have been telling you that since you were little."

"I know."

"D.J., there is no easy way for me to tell you what I am about to tell you."

"Tara said you had something to tell me. Just spit it out, Mom."

"Me and your brothers are moving to Florida with Marcus."

"Who the hell is Marcus?" I asked.

"He is the guy who I have been dating for the past year. He asked me to marry him and I said yes."

"I only met that nigga one or two times! What type of shit is this?"

"Watch your damn mouth! I am still you mother," she shouted.

I stormed out of the car and slammed the door. I couldn't believe she had just sprung that on me.

"D.J., don't walk away from me! Look, this is something that I have been giving thought to since the beginning of the summer."

"You are married to *us*," I shouted. "You gonna put another nigga in front of your kids now?"

"That's not fair, son. All I have done for the last ten years is everything and anything to make your and your brothers' lives easier. What about *my* happiness?" she asked.

I said nothing. I sat down on the porch and draped my face with the fitted cap I was wearing. She snatched the hat away and I noticed that tears began slowly trickling down her cheeks.

"Son, I almost had a heart attack when Tara called to

tell me that you and your brother were shot," she cried. "I'm not just doing this for me. I'm doing it for the safety of us all. You put us in this situation, so don't sit there with that stupid frown on your face. You going out there fooling with those hoodlums got your little brother shot, for Christ's sake!"

I continued to sit in silence as I stared at the ground. She was right. Everything that had happened was my fault. Truthfully, I was pissed, but as I sat and thought, it began to make sense.

"I'm sorry, Mom, I'm sorry. Maybe it is a good idea," I added.

"You three mean everything to me, D.J., and I would never let another man come between us."

"I know you wouldn't," I said.

"But you have to understand that my life just can't stop and I think it would be best for your brothers. This place just isn't safe anymore. Your brother has two holes in his back to prove it."

Even though she was making a great case for justifying why she wanted to uproot my brothers and go to Florida, I couldn't imagine not being able to visit my house on Delray Avenue. It wasn't really about her marrying Marcus. I just knew that life would never be the same if they moved away.

I soon realized that a change might be the best ther-
apy for us all. Nothing good was resulting from what I
had been doing that summer anyway.

It was easy to see that my desire for fast money had
taken me to a place that I really hadn't bargained for. At
that point and time, life lessons had a way of slapping
me in the face.

The money wasn't the root of the problem. People
like me who exploited others for personal gratification
and a few bucks were to blame. All of us were guilty as
charged.

SEVENTEEN

I kept myself locked up at Tara's house until I couldn't take it anymore. That was actually the only place comfortable to me after everything that had recently happened. When I brought up the news that my mom was moving to Florida, I was surprised that she was taking it so easily. It seemed like the life I knew was just so far out of reach.

My family was moving to Florida, I was leaving for the army in a couple of weeks. Tara was headed to graduate school in Virginia later in the fall. And Kev had already left for minicamp in Arizona. I figured Dre and Fat

Chris would be knocking on prison's door sooner than later if they didn't stop robbing folks. As for Joey and Bum, you could never tell what either of those dudes was going to do next. In reality, I couldn't even tell myself what I was going to do in my future. I guess Tara began to take notice.

"Baby, I know you have been through a lot this summer, but you have been walking around like a lost soul lately."

"I'm not a lost soul," I said, smiling. "I just have a lot on my mind, that's all."

"Like what?"

"Nothing in particular, life is just crazy," I returned.

"Well, D.J., it might get a little crazier."

"What do you mean by that?"

"My period is almost two weeks late."

"Stop playing games, Tara, you are on the pill. Plus, you know I pull out anyway."

"Boy, you don't always pull out, so stop lying," she said abruptly. "I have another confession, too."

"What now?" I asked.

"I haven't been taking my birth control pills."

"Why the fuck not?" I shouted furiously.

"Because I have been so stressed-out from all these things you've put me through that sometimes I just forget. After a while, that can accumulate and you can go back to being fertile."

A child was the last thing that I needed in my life. There was no way that I wasn't leaving, regardless of whether she was pregnant or not. I watched too many of my friends get caught up in similar situations.

"Well, you know what we gotta do," I said.

"Yes, take care of our child if I am indeed pregnant," she replied.

"Ain't gonna be no damn child! You're getting an abortion."

"No the hell I'm not!"

"I'm not gonna be trapped in that baby-mama-drama shit that Dre and other niggas go through," I uttered. "You can forget about that!"

"Do I look or seem like one of those dumb bitches, D.J.? I am your girlfriend, or did you forget? But you are still too worried about running around sticking your dick into anything that moves. You need to man up and stop acting like a little fucking boy!" she yelled.

"Don't come at me like that," I said angrily. "I'm a grown-ass man. If you're pregnant, then I will take care of my responsibilities, of course. I just thought I would be married to the girl who was having my baby."

"So I guess I'm just not marriage material," she said grudgingly.

"Maybe you're not."

As soon as I said that, I wished I could have had those three words back. She leaned back on her bed and began crying her eyes out. I tried to explain to her that I didn't really mean for the words to come out like that. It was too late, though. The damage was already done.

"Get the fuck out, D.J.!" she screamed.

"Look . . . I'm sorry, I didn't mean for . . . just calm down, please."

"Fuck you," she hollered. "Get out of my house right now or I'm calling my dad up here!"

"Tara, stop it right now!"

"Just GET OUT!" she shouted.

I grabbed my phone and slammed her bedroom door as I stormed out of her room. As I started my car, I asked myself how I managed to piss off the only person who was always in my corner.

Five minutes after I had left her house, my phone rang. She was ready for me to return—so I thought.

"Don't try to beg me to come back now," I answered.

"I never thought I would have to beg you, cutie," a soft voice said on the other end.

"What . . . who's this?"

"This is Maria . . . sounds like you and the wifey are having a little fight," she said.

"Nah, it's all good. What's up, shorty," I asked.

"You tell me, sweetie," she said. "I have been thinking about you a lot."

"Oh yeah, why is that?"

"Just come over to my house," she replied. "I want to cook you dinner and give you the rest of me before you leave."

"The rest of you?"

"Yes, the rest of me," she said. "You telling me you don't want it?"

I immediately had a flashback of the last time I saw her. I got aroused just thinking about how soft her lips were. For once, I was going to try to do the right thing. Tara had just kicked me out of her house ten minutes earlier and I knew that I wanted to go back. I didn't want to go spend time with another girl at a time like this.

God is watching, I thought to myself.

Then again, he forgave Adam after Eve coerced him to take a bite of the forbidden apple. I figured he would forgive me, too. Maria wasn't going to allow me to say no anyway. I don't think I wanted to say no, either. I liked her because she wasn't afraid to take contol.

"I live at the Cascades downtown," she said. "Across the street from the Capitol Building."

I paused for a second, but a power inside me took control. I guess I was listening to the other brain that most men think with, the one that always ends up getting us into trouble.

"I'm on my way," I replied.

"Just call me when you get outside, sweetie!"

"I will."

"See you when you get here."

My next stop was the Cascades . . .

EIGHTEEN

When Tara stepped outside to leave for work the next morning, her silver Toyota Camry was filled with fresh red and pink roses. The flowers were a good idea, but I had stooped to an all-time low to get them. While I was at Maria's condo, I learned that she made a living managing her father's flower shop. After our rendezvous came to a close, she took me to her store and blessed me with four dozen roses to give to Tara. I tried to pay her for them, but she would not accept any money from me. I had an extra set of keys to Tara's car, so I crept to her house early in the morning and put the roses inside.

I was already up mowing the lawn when Tara pulled up to my house. I could see her ivory white teeth glistening as she smiled before she exited the car. I knew she would be pleased. She loved roses too much not to be.

"Don't think just because you got me roses that you are off the hook, D.J."

"Get over here and gimme a hug! I'm sorry for hurting your feelings, babe," I said.

"Ewww, get away from me! You are all nasty and sweaty. I still have to go to work!"

"Even when I'm dirty, I'm still the flyest nigga you know," I said playfully.

"I have some news for you, babe."

"What now, Tara? Every time you say that shit lately, it's never good," I responded.

"Aunt Flo came last night!"

"Who the hell is Aunt Flo?"

"Aunt Flo is my period, stupid," she said, laughing. "It came last night at about three in the morning."

"Thank God!"

"I knew you would be jumping for joy," she replied. "I should have just made you sweat since you treated me like shit last night!"

I really did feel like doing a couple backflips. I loved Tara to death, but a baby at that point in my life was the wrong answer. I was still having trouble making the right decisions for me. I damn sure didn't want to start making them for a child, too.

"It's not even like that, babe. We both have so much to look forward to and I want to be able to take care of you and our kids before we have any."

"Oh, now we are going to start a family," Tara said sarcastically. "You were singing a different tune yesterday."

"I told you I didn't mean to say that shit. Let's go in the house so I can make it up to you," I continued anxiously.

"Eww, get out of here . . . you stink! I have to be at work in fifteen minutes. I gotta go, D.J."

"Call me when you get off," I said as I gently slapped her on her butt. "Love you."

"I love you more," she said as she closed the car door.

♦

I took my time doing the rest of the front yard. I think I was mowing extra slow because I knew that it was probably the last time I would ever cut the putrid-smelling grass at 100 Delray Avenue. The movers were scheduled to pack up the house in one week, so I had to enjoy ev-

ery minute of my time at the place I'd called home since
I was eleven years old.

I lounged around the house for the rest of day until
I grew tired of looking at the same surroundings. I still
had a good amount of cash hidden upstairs, so I decided
to go to the mall to get Korey a few things. I was spoil-
ing him ever since he had left the hospital. I felt bad because my youngest brother began to notice. This time,
however, I bought both of them a few pairs of sneakers,
as well as enough school clothes so they could start the
school year off. They shared clothing like two females,
so I knew they would be straight for a few months when
they got to Florida.

I felt awkward when I finally made it back home. It
was Friday night and my cell phone wasn't ringing at
all. It had not been for the past few weekends because
none of my friends had really been calling. As I sat on
the notorious bench on my porch, sipping a cold brew, I
realized that I missed every one of them.

♦

The weekend was over before I could blink. Nothing exciting, I just hung around the house with my little brothers and Tara. Everything was back to normal for a brief
moment, but that summer had already changed all of

our lives forever. My mom was so excited to leave that she wouldn't even let me, her firstborn son, rain on her parade. I swallowed my pride and took her fiancé out to dinner so I could let him know that I expected him to take good care of my folks. He seemed like a decent dude, but you could never judge a book by its cover. He knew that I'd be watching very closely.

It felt like I fell asleep that Sunday night and woke up Friday morning. To this day, I cannot account for the nights in between. They flew by so quickly. I was hoping that I was dreaming, but I was smacked by reality when a noisy semitruck pulled up in front of my house. The movers were there to take my family's belongings and all of our great memories, as well. To them, it was just another day on the job, but to me, it marked the end of an era. No longer would I be able to call the place that made me what I am home. We all agreed that there would never be another place like it.

I had to laugh to stop from crying.

NINETEEN

By midafternoon, half of the house was loaded onto the huge trailer. I felt that I should have been helping because they had been slaving since eight o'clock in the morning. It was lunchtime, so I decided to go buy a couple buckets of chicken so they could at least have a decent meal. Lord knows they deserved it. They were appreciative when I brought the chicken back, but when I wheeled over the cooler full of cold beer from the backyard, they looked at me like I was their savior.

"I know y'all probably ain't supposed to drink on the

job, but a couple of these might take the edge off," I said. "It's not getting any cooler out here."

The youngest guy on the porch was the first to grab one. I wasn't even sure if this dude was of age, but it really didn't matter. After everyone cracked a beer and got situated with their lunch, the guy in charge broke the silence.

"Is that your Cadillac?" asked the gray-haired supervisor.

This dude looked as old as my grandfather, but he was still out earning a living. He should have been somewhere living off Social Security, in my opinion.

"Yeah, that's my shit," I responded.

"That thing is tight! What year is it?"

"It's really an oh-two, but when people ask, I tell them it's an oh-four," I said. "Only people that really know about Caddies can tell the difference. I'm actually trying to get rid of it because I'm leaving next week."

"How much are you selling it for?"

"Make me an offer," I suggested.

"Hell, the more money I make, the more money my wife takes," he said sadly.

"I'm not even married yet and my girl takes all my cash, so I definitely feel your pain."

At first, I really didn't take a liking to this old man because he was just standing around while the younger workers were working tirelessly. After I talked to him, though, he seemed very down to earth. I could tell he was probably in his mid-sixties because he sounded out of whack when he attempted to use slang. The other workers and I would look at each other and laugh when he'd use words that he probably didn't even know the meaning of.

He let them break for about fifteen more minutes then put them back to work. Next, I went out back on the patio so I could just relax by myself. My mom left the kitchen and sat down at the table with me.

"D.J., why is it that every time I see you, you have a beer in your hand?"

"I'm just getting into my zone."

"Yeah . . . the drunk zone," she replied. "You're going to end up just like your daddy and your grandfather, a stone-cold alcoholic."

"Hold on, Mom . . . I've seen you drunk on a few occasions, too," I said, chuckling. "But I did catch Granddad at the Pussycat Lounge the other night, chasing some chick who was probably forty years younger than him."

"That fool ain't never gonna ever change," she replied. "What about your daddy?"

"You are my mom and my dad . . . you know that," I said.

"D.J., one day you are going to have to let it go. I know he left, but he has been trying to make it up to you ever since."

"I surely can't tell," I returned heatedly. "Sending money every month and a few birthday and Christmas presents over the years isn't enough in my book."

"He did what he could . . . maybe one day you two will sort things out."

"I won't hold my breath," I returned. "Besides, I had the coolest mom in the 'hood growing up. That's more than any kid can ask for."

My friends had always wished that they had a mom like mine. She didn't take any crap, but she never stopped us from having a good time. That's why my house was the spot where everything went down, no matter what day it was.

"You leave next week, son, are you getting excited?"

"Heck no! What's exciting about getting told what to do twenty-four/seven?" I asked.

"It's going to be good for you. A little discipline is something that you need anyway."

"The only reason I signed on the dotted line was to get my student loans paid off and to pocket my signing bonus," I said.

"Hell, you owe me half of that right now," she returned.

"What are you talking about, Mom? You never gave me ten grand!"

"Boy, you drive in the money I gave you every day!" she shouted.

I guess I had selective amnesia. There were plenty of months when she paid my car payment while I was up at school. Plus, she put a few thousand down on it, too, so maybe I did owe her ten stacks.

"That's all right, though. You can pay me back when you start making that 'Johnnie Cochran money.' Remember you told me that?"

"Yes, Mom, I remember," I replied. "You know I got you covered."

"I know, son, just stay out of trouble and the sky will be the limit for you. Okay, I'm done with you . . . my crab legs are finished! I'm going in the house to eat before they lose their flavor!"

She jumped up out of her chair like the crab legs were going to get up and run away. I was the only one in my family who hadn't gotten hit with the seafood gene, so I decided to stay put.

♦

I passed out on the patio for a few hours to sleep off my slight buzz. When I awoke, the house was empty. The movers, my mom, and my little brothers were gone. She left a note on the kitchen counter saying that she was staying at Marcus's house until she and my brothers left in two weeks.

"I guess I'm on my own," I said to myself.

I had been staying with Tara for the past couple of days anyway. As I walked upstairs to use the bathroom, I heard some loud banging on the front door. I wasn't expecting anybody and Tara was at a dinner for her mom's birthday. I had no idea who it was.

When I opened the door, Dre, Fat Chris, Bum, and Joey were all parlaying on the front porch. Seeing all of them was one of the best feelings in the world. Being around the League had that affect on all of us.

TWENTY

Most times, stubborn people refuse to throw their pride aside in order to make amends when it's time to settle differences. I know this because I used to have that type of personality. However, with everything that had gone down that summer, we all understood that life was more important. I knew why they had come to my mom's house that day. It certainly meant as much to them as it did to me.

"Damn, nigga, I can't believe your mom is really giving up the house, dog," Dre said morbidly.

"Word up, I busted my first nut in this joint," followed Bum.

"Remember back in the day when we used to call it 'the crackhouse' when your mom worked nights?" Joey said blissfully.

"How could I forget," Fat Chris said. "I probably hit the most broads up in here on the real. Y'all niggas wasn't putting up numbers like I was."

"Bullshit," said Dre. "Bitches wasn't feeling your fat, black ass back in the day," he added.

"I lived here! I was the one putting up numbers," I said. "None of y'all were on my level."

"Well, when we hit the Firefly tonight, we'll see who still got game," Dre said excitedly.

"Nah, I'm not fooling with the club tonight," I replied. "Tara is about to come through in a minute."

"Man, fuck that love bird shit tonight! You leave next week, dog!"

"I know, D.J., just bring her with you," Bum suggested.

"What I look like, bringing sand to the beach?" I said. "You the only loser that escorts his girl around like that. I'm bound to see somebody that I want to get with."

"You are leaving next week, though. Tara ain't letting

you out of her sight," said Joey. "She knows what we do when we get together."

Joey was absolutely right. There was no way that I could have told Tara that I was going out with the League and I only had a week before it was time for me to leave. I knew that I would have to take her if I wanted to go. I contemplated this for a second until I made my decision.

"Fuck it! I'm gonna just bring her," I said. "I bet I still have broads jocking me. You niggas might learn something if you study my swagger, so watch and learn!"

Just as I was finishing my sentence, Tara pulled into the driveway. She hopped out looking pretty as a peach, too, because she had just left her mom's dinner party. The form-fitting pink dress she had on complemented her cinnamon skin perfectly. This made me even more willing to take her to the club that night. She strutted up to the porch on her heels like she was on a runway. I was definitely digging her whole style.

"Damn, D.J., if I were you, I'd just stay home," said Fat Chris.

"Don't be eye fuckin' my girl, fat boy," I said.

"Where you think you going, babe?" Tara asked.

"We're all going to the Firefly tonight and I'm taking you with me."

"I don't want to be around all that cigarette smoke and drunk chicks looking to get screwed."

"Stop complaining! Normally I wouldn't even be taking you. It's against the pimp code," I said jokingly.

"Whatever, just know I'm not staying all night," she replied.

♦

Everyone else was already dressed, so I went to my trunk and scooped an outfit for the night. I told my boys that we would meet them at ten o'clock, so that gave Tara and me about an hour to burn. She was looking too good for me to give up this opportunity. As soon as my friends left, we went straight in the house.

To make a long story short, I had to grab some wet wipes out my car to clean up some spots on the carpet after we were finished. There was no furniture left, so the floor was my only option.

TWENTY-ONE

When Tara and I arrived at the Firefly, Dre and company were already in our velvet booth having drinks. Both of us could tell that they were tipsy already and it hadn't even reached eleven o'clock yet. I ordered a couple shots with a brew to chase and got Tara a Long Island iced tea. That was all she needed. One stiff drink always was enough for her.

"Nigga, it's some bitches up in here," said Dre. "Oh—sorry, Tara, we ain't used to having broads around when we're here."

"Dre, I don't care what you say! You ain't my man."

"Yeah, I know. You're D.J.'s problem!"

"Both of y'all shut up," I interrupted. "If you spent more time sipping, then you wouldn't have time to argue."

"Word up," said Bum. "But fuck the drinks, I'm getting on the floor."

"Don't get hurt, nigga," Fat Chris said, snickering.

"You know Bum is dance fever," shouted Joey.

We all focused our attention on Bum as he grinded on some chick in the middle of the packed dance floor. She was thicker than a McDonald's milk shake, but I couldn't let Tara see that I was looking as hard as everyone else. We watched as she threw everything she had at him, but Bum wasn't a slouch when it came to his dance game. We were sure that he used to watch videos to pick up moves because every week he came up with a different routine. I was actually having a good time even though I had dragged Tara with me. Surprisingly, my boys were just chilling, which was a shock also. It wasn't one of the crazy nights like usual—no pouring drinks on broads or getting into fights. Things took an interesting turn as they always had around those times. I spotted a chick staring directly at me from the bar. Initially, I couldn't tell who it was, but as she began approaching, my stomach filled with a thousand butterflies. When she finally made it to the table, none of us knew what to expect. It was Maria.

"Hey D.J., what's up, everybody?"

"I'm good, just chilling with my people before I hit the road," I replied.

"Oh, you must be Tara. I have heard so much about you."

"Is that right," said Tara as she rolled her eyes.

"Yeah, she works at the flower shop where I bought your roses from," I said nervously.

"I hope you liked them, I cut them myself," said Maria.

"Yeah, they were very nice. Thank you."

"You got a good man, girl, don't let him get away!"

I didn't understand what was going on at all. She kept making small talk with Tara like they were friends or something. Luckily, Dre started running interference so Tara wouldn't think anything. I was hoping that this broad wasn't going to spill the beans. I knew that at any moment, my night could come crashing down.

"Well, it has been nice seeing you! Be safe in the army," Maria said jovially. "Make sure you come to my shop if you ever need anything, girl."

"Where is your shop at? I'm coming through tomorrow," followed Dre.

"I hope you're coming to buy flowers because that's all I'm selling," said Maria. "I'm not looking for a man, honey."

"We'll just have to see about that," returned Dre.

"Yeah . . . yeah . . . yeah," she said as she pivoted and marched off.

◆

I had to force myself not to stare as she walked away. I couldn't believe that things went as smooth as they did. I didn't know what to expect, but Maria surely played her part. Things could have gotten real ugly, but again, she wasn't your average chick. It didn't seem like Tara suspected anything and that was all I was worried about.

"She was nice," said Tara.

"That ass was nice, too," Fat Chris added.

"Is that all y'all think about is having sex with different women all the time?"

"Pretty much," said Joey.

"I can't wait until some young boys are chasing your daughters around trying to stick their little peepees in them," she said, laughing.

"I'll beat a little boy's ass like he stole something if I catch one trying to get some from one of my daughters," said Dre.

We spent the next two hours talking about what everybody had in store for the future. I kept drinking until I started to slur my words and that was when Tara had had enough. Just for the sake of not arguing, I stopped drinking and at about one o'clock, she was ready to leave.

"I'm ready to go, D.J."

"That's why we don't bring chicks with us, y'all can't hang," said Dre.

"Go home to your baby's mom or something," returned Tara.

"Which one, I have a few," he replied.

"I'm tired anyway, my niggas," I said. "I'm staying at her house, too, so we can't stroll in too late. Mr. Lewis ain't going for that shit!"

"Make sure you drive, Tara. This nigga D.J. is drunk," said Bum.

"D.J. will be passed out by the time we get home. He knows I'm driving."

"Hit me up tomorrow sometime," I said as I stood up.

We all slapped hands before Tara rushed me to the car. She quickly snatched the keys out of my hand before I could even blink. I had already gotten one DUI, there was no reason to risk getting another. She kept telling me she hated my friends as we got in the car, so

I turned the music up as loud as I could stand it. Normally, I didn't let her touch my CD player, but as we drove off, she slipped in some of her music because she complained that she didn't feel like listening to any hip-hop.

I was drunk anyway. A little R&B wasn't going to kill me. . . .

TWENTY-TWO

"**W**ake your drunk ass up, D.J.," Tara said as we merged onto the highway. "You ain't been in the car ten minutes and you're already passed out!"

"I'm not sleeping, baby, I'm just resting my eyes."

"Resting your eyes, yeah right," she replied. "You're probably over there daydreaming about Little Miss Flower Girl from the club."

"What's wrong with Maria? She gave me a discount on the roses I bought for you . . . don't think they were cheap."

"She just seemed a little too friendly to me. How did you pay her?"

"With cash, Tara, what do you think?"

"Yeah . . . I bet."

I was trying my best to change the conversation despite my victory over the close call at the club. Even though I was a little more relaxed, Tara kept hounding me like she was fishing for something. I really believe that girl had a sixth sense, but not for dead people; rather, for broads who'd had sex with her man. Finally, she let it go when I told her that I didn't want to spend my last week arguing over some worthless chick I purchased flowers from. If only she knew . . .

"You gonna give me a massage when we get home, babe?"

"Why do I always have to give you a massage?" she asked. "When are you gonna give *me* one?"

"C'mon, Tara, I work hard for a living. My body needs TLC."

"Shut up, boy! You haven't worked all summer," she added. "You're lucky you stopped messing with Dre and them before you got yourself into trouble."

"College boys don't get in real trouble. There are enough criminals in the streets to keep the pigs occupied. The police got better shit to do than fuck with a college grad that's going to serve their country."

"You're going to the army, D.J., that's jail in itself," she countered.

"Shut up and give me a kiss," I said as I pulled her toward me.

"Stop it, I'm trying to drive!" she shouted.

We made it to Tara's house about ten minutes later. As soon as we stepped into her bedroom, we plopped down on her feather-filled mattress top. That was one of the reasons I loved staying at her house. It felt like you were sleeping on a cloud. It had been a long day and we were both exhausted.

"Are you going to sleep, baby?" I asked.

"Yeah . . . I'm tired. Plus, as tipsy as you are, you probably can't even get it up!"

"Yeah right," I said, laughing. "You know what happens when I give you the whiskey dick."

"Not tonight. Just hold me for once."

"Okay . . . but tomorrow morning it's on!"

"Whatever you want, babe," she said, yawning.

"Good night."

"Don't be surprised if you feel something poking you later on tonight," I said as I stripped down under the comforter.

"Just go to sleep, D.J."

I knew that my time was really winding down. I had to cherish every moment that I had with my family, Tara, and the League. I could have prevented a lot of the things that happened that summer, but life was beginning to return to normal. Finally, I would get a good night's sleep.

TWENTY-THREE

The next morning, Tara and I were awakened by an aggressive knock on her bedroom door. It was still dim within the room so I knew that the sun was just rising. Another flurry of knocking continued but this time, it was accompanied by the voice of Tara's mother.

"D.J. . . . D.J., you need to put some clothes on now and get downstairs," Mrs. Lewis shouted through the door.

"What the hell? Tara, wake up," I said. "Your mom is

telling me I need to put on some clothes and go down-stairs."

"Well, go ahead, babe," she replied in a cranky voice.

I had no idea what was so urgent that Tara's mother had to wake me up so early. I shuffled to the bathroom to brush my teeth before I slipped on my clothes. As I walked out of her bedroom, I could hear chatter com-ing from the kitchen as I made my way down the stairs. When I got to the bottom of the steps, I froze. I definitely didn't like what I saw.

"Good morning, son. You are certainly not the easiest gentleman to catch up with."

I paused for what seemed like an eternity. A uni-formed police officer and another dressed in civilian clothing were standing in the middle of the kitchen. The uniformed officer was a stereotypical cop—white, heavyset, and suffering from major hair loss. He was the one doing all the talking. The black cop wouldn't even look me in my face. For a split second, I thought that I recognized him from somewhere. Mrs. Lewis was seated at the kitchen table with a look on her face that I could not begin to describe.

"For what reason would you need to catch up with me?"

"I think you know the answer to the question," he replied.

"If I knew the answer, then I wouldn't be asking," I said emphatically.

"You need to straighten up and answer the man's questions," demanded Mrs. Lewis.

"A friend of yours named Andre Banks was arrested last night and your name came up. We are going to have to escort you to the station to ask you a few questions," he added.

"It's eight o'clock in the morning, I'm not going to nobody's police station," I uttered. "You can ask me what you have to ask me right here, right now."

"That's a negative, you don't have a choice in the matter," said the black cop.

"You jakes ain't got nothing better to do than embarrass me at my girlfriend's home," I said. "Shouldn't you be somewhere fighting crime?"

"Son, you have enough things on your plate as it is. You wanna play hardball, huh? We can slap you with more charges if you like."

"Things . . . what things do I have on my plate?" I replied. "I haven't done anything. I'm going back upstairs because if you had anything on me then you would have arrested me already. I was a prelaw minor, I know my rights."

"I'm confused," said Mrs. Lewis.

"Mrs. Lewis, I'm sorry for the rude awakening," I replied quickly. "These cops don't have anything better to do but harass people, as you can see."

"This is nonsense, you are coming with us and that's final! Take him down, Mason!"

I turned around, walked through the breezeway toward the steps. Before I knew it, both officers were wrestling me to the ground in the living room. I wouldn't have resisted, but they had me in a position that was making it difficult for me to breathe.

"You brought this on yourself, buddy!"

"You have the right to remain silent! Anything you say—"

"Get the hell up off me, I can't breathe!" I shouted.

"Officer, he is a good kid," said Mrs. Lewis as she darted out of the kitchen. "He just graduated from college a few months ago! Why are you doing this to him?"

"Ma'am, then he must not be who you think he is," shouted one of the officers. "He is facing up to twenty-five years in jail for multiple charges to include armed robbery, as well as several counts of conspiracy and reckless endangerment."

"Oh my God, D.J., is what they are saying true?"

Before I could respond, the officers managed to toss me outside. Seconds later, Tara burst out of the door barely dressed, crying and demanding answers. As they shoved me in the back of the squad car, we communicated our last words before the cop vigorously slammed the door.

"What the hell is going on?" she cried.

"Tara, call my mom and come down to the police station!"

"Sir, what did he . . . why are you doing this to him?"

"Ma'am, get away from the car, *now!*"

"D.J., I don't know what to do!"

"Just call my mom and meet me downtown," I yelled from the back of the car.

As we pulled off, I gazed through the squad car's back window. Tara fell to her knees in the driveway as her mom hustled over to comfort her. After glancing at my reflection in the window, I asked myself if what was happening was even real. I had wished that I was having the worst dream I'd ever experienced. As I readjusted my hands to relieve the tightness of the handcuffs, every day from that summer flashed through my mind in a matter of seconds. During a ride that felt like forever, I contemplated what I was going to be faced with once I arrived at the police station. My nervousness had taken total control of me. My body was going crazy, but in my mind everything was clear.

I knew I was fucked.

TWENTY-FOUR

Upon arrival at the police station, the officers quickly hurled me into an interrogation room. As I glanced around the small box, I felt like I was in a scene from a movie. There was nothing in the room but a shoddy old table, a metal chair that appeared to be two sittings from collapsing, and three walls covered with penciled graffiti.

"Sit your ass down and don't move," huffed the black cop. "I love when we bring in guys like you who think they're tough. Act tough now, guy! I'll slap that smirk right off your face."

"You ain't nothing but that white cop's little fuck boy! Whose side are you on, nigga?"

"I'm on everybody's side that you and your home-boys robbed. You're lucky you boys ain't dead yet. I wish y'all would've ran up on me," he said. "All you punks would be in a casket right now."

When I first laid eyes on him at Tara's house, I had a feeling that I recognized him. As I stared him down in the dimly lit room, my memory finally caught up with me. On one of my visits to the District, he was leaving as I was going in. I knew it was him because I remembered how Tony bragged that he had just charged him nine grand for a bracelet that cost him almost nothing. I should have known he was an undercover cop. What other sane individual would spend nine thousand on a bracelet worth not even half that? If anyone was going to spend that kind of money on jewelry, they'd be smart enough to know if they were getting ripped off.

"I know who are you are," I said. "You can't be from around here because nobody from this 'hood would stoop low enough to be an undercover snitch."

"It don't matter where I'm from . . . what matters is where you gonna be spending the next ten years of your life," he replied. "You fucked yourself, young fella!"

If I didn't still have those cuffs on, I probably would

have charged him. Just as I began to respond, the door to the room opened abruptly. When I noticed who it was, I was both relieved and terrified at the same time. It was Detective Kinard.

"I'll take it from here, Detective Mason," said Kinard as he signaled for him to leave the room. "I told you that if you didn't keep your nose clean that I was going to crush you," he said. "You do realize that you put yourself into a situation that's going to change your life forever."

"Have you talked to my mom yet?"

"Yes, son, she is on her way right now, but Mommy can't help you this time. I know your mom told you that we were all over this case. Everyone involved with the robberies or anything else is going to burn."

"I don't know what you're talking about."

"I assume there is no use asking you if there was any other personnel involved other than you and Mr. Banks?"

"I don't know what you're talking about. Dre is my good friend, but that's as far as it goes. I don't know what he is involved in and y'all keep talking about armed robbery. I never robbed anyone."

"Is that right?" he returned. "I find that problematic because Tony Marchioni begs to differ."

"I don't know anybody named Tony Marchioni, either."

"Yes, you do . . . we have him in custody, too. He owns the Diamond District, the shop that you used to take the embezzled jewelry to. Now does his name ring a bell?"

I sat staring at the glass mirror on the left side of the room in silence. I was sure that there were other officers watching as he was questioning me. Detective Kinard knew it all. I had no idea what Dre had told him, but it didn't really matter. He didn't need me to admit to anything. It was clear that I was going down.

"He was arrested on charges unrelated to your case, but as a part of his plea bargain, he agreed to testify against all of you in exchange for a lesser sentence."

"Nah, Tony ain't no rat," I said under my breath.

"The game changes when you put a little pressure on somebody, son. That's something that life will teach you real soon."

"You can put as much pressure on me as you want! I know what I did and didn't do," I replied.

"I told you weeks ago to tell me the truth about what was going on," he said. "Now I cannot help you. I did everything within my power."

I finally broke down and buried my face in between

my hands. That was the first time a grown man ever witnessed me cry. All I could think about was how I was going to face my mom and Tara. I thought about the heartbreak that the situation was going to cause both of them.

"Man up, D.J., everyone makes their own decisions. It's taking responsibility for them that is the hard part," he said in a muffled voice. "Take a few minutes to get yourself together. I will be back in soon. I'm being paged by the captain."

"But Detective Kinard . . . ?"

He slammed the door behind him as I tried to get more answers. Now, it was just me, my thoughts, and an empty room. I miserably buried my head between my arms. I didn't even want to look at my reflection in the mirror. I repeatedly asked myself why I was so stupid. I knew I should not have taken that jewelry to Tony in the first place. I shouldn't even have accepted it from Dre. Granted, I never put a gun to anyone, but I was the catalyst for the entire operation, so that made me just as guilty.

As I dug deeper into my twisted mind, I came to the realization that I had been fooling myself all along. I was the worst person out of everyone involved. For the entire summer, I had not been accepting responsibility for what I was the cause of. It was me that decided to go to the Diamond District. It was me that put his closest friends in harm's way while I sat back and enjoyed the fruits of their dangerous labor. It was my fault that my brother's back had gotten filled with bullets.

Quite frankly, I was at the root of everybody's misfortune. Even worse, I knew that the only reason I really stopped the scheme was because I was worried about my own welfare, not anyone else's. Jail was probably the best place for anyone who used manipulation to corrupt everyone around him. I was to blame for forcing every person I cared about into a game where everybody ended up losing. At that particular moment, I believe I had enough self-hatred in my heart to take my own life. Luckily, I had no means to do so.

I wished that I could take back everything that I had done that summer. It was way too late, though. I stood up and began pacing around the room. I had to prepare myself for the worst because I knew that was what I was going to face. All I could do was think about my mom, my brothers, and Tara. Detective Kinard came back to the room approximately an hour later. I didn't know what to expect.

"Sit down, D.J. I spent thirty minutes of the last hour speaking to the day judge," he said. "Because you were facing multiple felony charges, the judge would not per-mit bail."

Game over, I thought. I didn't need to hear anything else.

"Thanks for your help, Detective Kinard. I made my bed . . . I'm the one who has to sleep in it. Has Tara or Mom made it yet? I would at least like to see them be-fore I get locked down."

"Of course, they are both here," he replied.

I stood up and scrubbed my face with the sleeve of my T-shirt so neither of them would know I was crying. I knew that I had to suck it up because they were the ones who were going to be devastated.

"Sit back down, son! Being that you are an Ivy Leaguer, I figured you would have learned something while you were in college," said Detective Kinard. "You probably didn't pay attention in class while you were at Penn, did you?"

"Some classes I did, some I didn't," I replied. "What does that have to do with anything?"

"If you would have paid attention to me a minute ago, you'd have understood that I said I was talking to the judge about getting bail set for charges that you *were* facing. You aren't facing any criminal charges anymore," he uttered reluctantly.

"What? What are you saying?"

"I also had the opportunity to speak with Captain Riggs. Apparently, in a sworn statement, Mr. Banks admitted to every single robbery that was tracked in this case. He told the other detectives that you didn't have anything to do with it and that the only thing you did was introduce him to Marchioni. He claims that is the only time you were at the Diamond District that he knows of. If this is true, then you will walk out of here a free man," he added.

I had a choice to make. Either way, no decision was going to be the right one. If I said it was true, then I could walk out of the station and leave one of my best friends to face condemnation alone. If I said no and came clean, we'd both be finished. For a moment, I thought he was just trying to get me to snitch on Dre. Until this day, I don't know if I made the right decision.

"It's the . . . that's the truth," I said unwillingly.

"Captain Riggs instructed me to lock you up if I suspected that you were lying," returned Detective Kinard. "Luckily, I don't work like that. I'll let *God* decide. He is the judge that everybody has to sit in front of one day. One more thing. After writing his sworn statement, Andre wrote a letter to you. He begged that I make sure you got it before you left, so here it is."

He reached inside of his blazer and tossed a beige envelope onto the table. I felt like I could hardly speak.

"Can you . . . will you take these handcuffs off then?"

"I guess so. You are no longer under arrest."

I stood up as he jiggled the cuffs off my wrists. I hadn't taken my eyes off the envelope since it hit the table. I looked Detective Kinard in his hardened face once more and said the most sincere "thank you" that has ever left my mouth.

"Don't thank me, just don't let me ever see you again under these circumstances," he said and began to walk out the door. "Next time, you won't be so fortunate. You got off . . . I don't know if you deserve to . . . but you did."

Tears began rolling down my face once again. I snatched the envelope off the table and sat on the dust-ridden floor of the lifeless interrogation room. Next, I scooted back into the corner so I could not be seen through the transparent mirror. I wiped my face and began to read the already tear-soaked letter.

I knew I had just thrown the world on Dre's shoulders. I wasn't moving until I was finished reading what he had to say.

TWENTY-FIVE

Yo D.J.,

By the time you read this letter, the jakes probably gonna have your boy under the jail. I decided to confess to all this shit because it was no sense in all of us going down. Plus, you know I'm a jailhouse vet, doing a little time ain't gonna phase me. Prison ain't no place for a nigga like you, though, dog. I'm not saying that you can't hold your own, but you would have been a college boy scorned up in this hell. I'm gonna have a lot of time to think now that I'm up in here. Maybe, I will understand all that preaching you was doing this summer. I don't even listen to T. D. Jakes or the pastor at my mom's church so what made you think I was gonna listen to you? My whole life, I've had to hustle. I got five kids and three different baby moms so dealing with all that pressure is not easy. I hope you understand that. You can barely get a job with only a high school diploma these days and if you do, it don't pay you shit. I can't do shit for my kids on minimum wage. That's why I was always hustling. I don't have a college degree. All I got is street smarts. I do know that you are the smartest nigga I ever met. I have always looked up to you because you keep it real but you still take care of your priorities. I should have learned that by watching you, but I guess I didn't. I know you are gonna be something one day. For real, you already are something. I know it's not easy for a nigga to finish college. Especially, in our fucked-up educational system where they set tuition so only people who got money can afford it. Now, I realize that money ain't everything. It's just a piece of paper. When you in jail, cigarettes are like cash. People get they asses whipped over boxes of candy bars and cartons of cancer sticks on the regular. On the outside, I guess money isn't really what matters. It's what it brings to you. It didn't bring me shit but a parole violation, more felonies, and probably ten years in prison depending on what the judge gives me. You the only person in this world I can count on so I want you to do something for me. Please look after my kids while I'm in here. Make sure their moms do what they supposed to do and if they need something, get it for them. I will pay you back double when I get out, no matter how much it costs you. I know they will be all right if you looking after them. Other than that, I'm just going to do my time. I needed a long vacation anyway. Oh yeah, put a wedding ring on Tara's finger. She is a good girl and she loves you. Leave all them other girls alone so you don't get caught up like I did. Also, send me some money from time to time so I can buy deodorant and shit, too. And tell the rest of the League that I said to write me sometime and don't forget to tell your moms I said wussup and that I'm sorry for all this. Last but not least, be at the gate with a case of beer the day I get released. Don't change your phone number either, 'cause when you get a call from the correctional facility, you know it's gonna be me. I'm gonna tough this shit out, just make sure you hold it down on the outside and I'll see you in few years. I hope you didn't let them pressure you into admitting shit because if you did, your life is gonna be fucked up just like mine. I'm hoping that a college nigga would be smarter than that. I guess you were right when you said "karma is a bitch." Too bad I realized it too late. Keep in touch . . .

Stay Real,
Andre

TWENTY-SIX

My reply:

Dre,

By the time you get this letter, I will be Uncle Sam's property. I really don't know where to begin, dog. I feel like I owe my life to you. It has been five days since I left the police station and I can't seem to get right. All this shit was my fault and you still took all the blame. I am supposed to leave tomorrow at six in the morning, but I don't even know if I want to go. I feel like I betrayed you. I think I read your letter one hundred times since last week and every time I read it, it fucks my head up. Every day I look in the mirror and get angry at myself. The only thing that keeps me from going crazy is that you asked me to look out for your kids. It's my fault that you are in there alone, so best believe I am going to do everything within my power to make them comfortable. I am going to treat them like they were my own. They won't need for anything, I promise you that. I hollered at the League and gave them the address to the jail, so you should be getting letters from everybody. They all asked me if you mentioned their names in your confession. I almost slapped every last one of them. They know you aren't a snitch. I still can't believe what you did, but I understand why. You say that you look up to me, but in reality, I look up to you. You taught me the true meaning of sacrifice. I don't think another person in this world would have done what you did. You are right about Tara, too. I know she is the one. I just have to sow my wild oats before I make that commitment. Don't think that just because you didn't go to college that I am any better than you, either. You taught me something about sacrifice that is more valuable than any college class I have ever taken. I bet there are thousands of niggas locked up that have something to offer society. Maybe people should be going to prison visits instead of Tuesday and Thursday classes. I have a lot of people depending on me, so I can't afford to fail. It all comes down to making the right decisions, whether you are a college boy, a street nigga, or a CEO of a million-dollar enterprise. They lock people like us up all the time for years, but set people free that have misled and robbed people for millions. Look at Martha Stewart. I can't hate on her, though. She is a hustler just like anybody else. I'm done preaching to you, dog. I'm going to send you a couple books that I would like you to read. I might even write one that tells our story, you never know. Just realize that I got your back until I stop breathing. Tara wants me to tell you to keep your head up and that she is going to make sure your daughters always have enough clothes and things. My mom's crib is officially closed up. She put it on the market to be sold today. That's all right, though, because when you get out, the new 100 Delray Avenue will be wherever my house is. There will always be a room open for you, too. I'm not one for the sentimental-type shit, but I love you, dog. Thanks for giving me the chance to live my life. There is no way I can ever pay you back. I will hold it down on the outside and don't hesitate to let me know if you need something. Keep the letters coming, too. I'm definitely going to write to you as much as I can to keep you up on what's going on in the streets. It won't hurt if you pick up the Bible a little bit, as well. I went to church for the first time in months last Sunday and I felt like the preacher was talking straight to me. They say God works in mysterious ways. Hopefully, he still has us in his plan somewhere. Do some push-ups and pull-ups, too, dog. When I come visit you, I want to see some muscles on that skinny frame of yours. It's time for us to start walking the right path because the journey that we have been on led all of us astray. Be strong and keep your head up. Oh yeah, don't drop the soap . . .

Your Boy,

D.J.

P.S. League till we die . . .

TURN THE PAGE FOR EXCERPTS
OF MORE G-UNIT BOOKS
by 50 Cent

DERELICT

By 50 Cent and Relentless Aaron

DERELICT: Shamefully negligent in not having done what one should have done.

Prison: One of the few places on earth where sharks sleep, and where *"You reap what you sow."*

𝕿he note that Prisoner Jamel Ross attached, with his so called "urgent request," to see the prison psychotherapist was supposed to appear desperate: *"I need to address some serious issues because all I can think about is killing two people when I leave here. Can you help me!"* And that's all he wrote. But even more than the anger, revenge, and redemption Jamel was ready to bring back to the streets, he also had the prison's psych as a target; a target of his lust. And that was a more pressing issue at the moment.

"**As far back** as I can remember life has been about growing pains," he told her. "I've been through the phases of a liar in my adolescence, a hustler and thug in my teens, and an all-out con man in my twenties. Maybe it was just my instincts to acquire what I considered resources—by whatever means necessary, but it's a shame that once you get away with all of those behaviors, you become good at it, like some twisted type of talent or profession. Eventually even lies feel like the truth . . .

". . . I had a good thing going with *Superstar*. The magazine. The cable television show. Meeting and comingling with the big name celebrities and all. I was positioned to have the biggest multimedia company in New York; the biggest to focus on black entertainment exclusively. BET was based in Washington at the time, so I had virtually no competition. Jamel Ross, the big fish in a little pond . . .

"And of course I got away with murder, figuratively, when Angel—yes, the singer with the TV show and all her millions of fans—didn't go along with the authorities, including her mother, who wanted to hit me with child molestation, kidnapping, and other charges. I was probably dead wrong for laying with that girl before she turned eighteen. But Angel was a very grown-up seventeen-year-old. Besides, when I hit it she was only a few months shy from legal. So, gimme a break.

"In a strange way, fate came back to get my ass for all of my misdeeds. All of my pimp-mania. That cable company up in Connecticut (with more than four hundred stations and fifty-five million subscribers across the country) was purchased by an even larger entity. It turned my life around when that happened; made my brand-new, million-dollar contract null and void. There was no way that I could sue anyone because lawyers' fees are incredible and my company overextended itself with the big celebrations, the lavish spending, and the increased staff; my living expenses, including the midtown penthouse, and the car notes, and maintenance for Deadra and JoJo—my two lovers, at the time—were in excess of eleven thousand a month. Add that to the overhead at *Superstar* and, without a steady stream of cash flowing, I had an ever-growing monster on my hands.

"One other thing, both Deadra and JoJo became pregnant, so now I would soon have four who depended on me as the sole provider. Funny, all of this wasn't an issue when things were lean. When the sex was good and everyone was kissing my ass. Now, I'm the bad guy because the company's about to go belly-up."

With a little more than two years left to his eighty-four-month stretch, Jamel Ross finally got his wish, to sit and spill his guts to Dr. Kay Edmonson, the psychotherapist at Fort Dix—the Federal Correctional Institution that was a fenced-in forty-acre plot on the much bigger Fort Dix Army Base. Fort Dix was where Army reservists went to train, and simultaneously where felons did hard time for crimes gone wrong. With so many unused acres belonging to the government during peacetime, someone imagined that perhaps a military academy or some other type of income-producing entity would work on Fort Dix as well. So they put a prison there.

The way that Fort Dix was set up was very play it by ear. It was a growing project where new rules were implemented along the way. Sure, there was a Bureau of Prisons guidebook with regulations for both staff and convicts to follow. However, that BOP guidebook was very boilerplate, and it left the prison administrators in a position in which they had to learn to cope and control some three thousand offenders inside of the fences of what was the largest Federal population in the system. It was amazing how it all stayed intact for so long.

"On the pound" nicknames were appreciated and accepted since it was a step away from a man's birth name, or "government name," which was the name that all the corrections officers, administrative staff, and of course the courts, used when addressing convicts. So, on paper Jamel's name was Jamel

Ross. On paper, Jamel Ross was not considered to be a person, but a "convict" with the registration number 40949–054, something like the forty thousandth prisoner to be filtered through the Southern District of New York. The "054" being the sort of area code in his prison ID number. He was sentenced by Judge Benison in October of 1997, committed to eighty-four months—no parole, and three years probation. The conviction was for bank robbery. However, on appeal, the conviction was "adjusted" since there was no conclusive evidence that Jamel had a weapon. Nevertheless, Jamel certainly *did* have a weapon and fully intended to pull off a robbery, with a pen as his weapon. So, the time he was doing was more deserved than not.

But regardless of Jamel's level of involvement, it was suddenly very easy for him to share himself since he felt he had nothing to lose. It was much easier to speak to a reasonably attractive woman, as if there was good reasoning for the things he did and why. So, he went on explaining all of his dirty deeds to "Dr. Kay" Edmondson, as if this were a confessional where he'd be forgiven for his sins. And why not? She was a good-listening, career-oriented female. She was black and she wasn't condescending like so many other staff members were. And when she called him "Jamel," as opposed to "Convict Ross," it made him imagine they had a tighter bond in store.

"So this dude—I won't say his name—he let me in on his check game. He explained how one person could write a check for, say, one hundred grand, give it to a friend, and even if the money isn't there to back up the check, the depositor could likely withdraw money on it before it is found to be worthless. It sounded good. And I figured the worst case scenario would be to deny this and to deny that. . . ."

"They don't verify the check? I mean, isn't that like part of the procedure before it clears?" Kay generally did more talking than this when a convict sat before her. Except she was finding his story, as well as his in-depth knowledge of things, so fascinating.

"See, that's the thing. If the check comes from the same region, or if it's from the other side of the world, it still has to go through a clearing house, where all of the checks from *all* of the banks eventually go. So that takes like a couple of days. But banks—certain banks—are on some ol' 'we trust you' stuff, and I guess since they've got your name and address 'n' stuff, they do the cash within one or two days."

"Really?"

"Yup. They will if it's a local check from a local bank. And on that hundred grand? The bank will let loose on the second day. I'll go in and get the money when the dam breaks. . . ."

"And when the bank finds out about the check being no good?"

"I play dumb. I don't know the guy who wrote the check. Met him only twice, blah blah blah. I sign this little BS affidavit and *bang*—I'm knee-deep in free money."

Dr. Kay wagged her head of flowing hair and replied, "You all never cease to amaze me. I mean *you,* as in the convict here. I hear all sorts of tricks and shortcuts and—"

"Cons. They're cons, Doctor Kay."

"Sure, sure . . ." she somehow agreed.

"But it's all a dead-end, ya know? Like, once you get money, it becomes an addiction, to the point that you forget your *reasons* and *objectives* for getting money in the first place."

"Did *you* forget, Jamel?"

"Did I? I got *so deep* in the whole check thing that it became my new profession."

"Stop playin'."

"I'm for real. I started off with my own name and companies, but then, uhh . . ." Jamel hesitated. He looked away from the doctor. "I shouldn't really be tellin' you this. I'm ramblin'."

"You don't have to if you don't want to, but let me remind you that what you say to me in our sessions is confidential, unless I feel that you might cause harm to yourself or someone else, or if I'm subpoenaed to testify in court."

"Hmmm." Jamel deliberated on that. He wondered if the eighty-four month sentence could be enhanced to double or triple, or worse. He'd heard about the nightmares, how bragging while in prison was a tool that another prisoner could use to shorten his own sentence. "Informants" they called them. And just the *thought* of that made Jamel promise himself that he wouldn't say a thing about the weapon and the real reason he caught so much time.

"Off the record, Jamel . . ."

"Oooh, I like this 'off-the-record' stuff." Jamel rubbed his hands together and came to the edge of the couch from his slouched position.

"Well, to put your mind at ease, I haven't *yet* received a subpoena for a trial."

Jamel took that as an indication of secrecy and that he was supposed to have confidence in her. But he proceeded with caution as he went on explaining about the various bank scams, the phony licenses and bogus checks.

The doctor said, "Wow, Jamel. That's a hell of a switch. One day you're a television producer, a publisher, and a ladies' man, and the next—"

The phone rang.

"I'm sorry." Dr. Kay got up from her chair, passed Jamel and circled her desk. It gave him a whiff of her perfume, and that only had him to pay special attention to her calves. There was something about a woman's calves that got him excited. Or didn't. But Dr. Kay's calves *did*. As she took her phone call, Jamel wondered if she did the StairMaster bit, or if she ran in the mornings. Maybe she was in the military like most of these prison guards claimed. Was she an aerobics instructor at some point in her life? All of those ideas were flowing like sweet Kool-Aid in Jamel's head as he thought and wondered and imagined.

"Could you excuse me?" Dr. Kay said.

"Sure," said Jamel, and he quickly stepped out of the office and shut the door behind him. Through the door's window he tried to cling to her words. It seemed to be a business call, but that was just a guess. A hope. It was part of Jamel's agenda to guess and wonder what this woman or that woman would be like underneath him, or on top of him. After all, he was locked up and unable to touch another being. So, his imaginings were what guided him during these seven years. He'd take time to look deep into a woman, and those thoughts weren't frivolous but anchored and supported by his past. Indeed, sex was a major part of his life from a teen. It had become a part of his lifestyle. Women. The fine ones. The ones who weren't so fine, but whom he felt he could "shape up and get right." Dr. Kay was somewhere in between those images. She had a cute face and an open attitude. Her eyes smiled large and compassionate. She was cheeky when she smiled, with lips wide and supple. Her teeth were bright and indicated good hygiene.

And Dr. Kay wasn't built like an *Essence* model or a dancer in a video. She was a little thick where it mattered, and she had what Jamel considered to be "a lot to work with."

Big-breasted with healthy hips, Dr. Kay was one of a half dozen women on the compound who were black. There were others who were Hispanic and a few more who were white. But of those who were somehow accessible, Dr. Kay nicely fit Jamel's reach. And to reach her, all he had to do was make the effort to trek on down to the psychology department, in the same building as the chapel and the hospital. All you had to do was express interest in counseling. Then you had to pass a litmus test of sorts, giving your reason for needing counseling. Of course, Dr. Kay wasn't the only psychotherapist in the department. There were one or two others. So Jamel had to hope and pray that his interview would 1) be with Dr. Kay Edmonson, and 2) that his address would be taken sincerely, not as just another sex-starved convict who wanted a whiff or an eyeful of the available female on the compound.

Considering all of that, Jamel played his cards right and was always able to have Dr. Kay set him up for a number of appointments. It couldn't be once a week; the doctor-convict relationship would quickly burn out at that rate. But twice a month was a good start, so that she could get a grip on who (and what) he was about. Plus, his visits wouldn't be so obvious as to raise any red flags with her boss, who, as far as Jamel could tell, really didn't execute any major checks and balances of Kay's caseload. Still, it was the other prisoners at Fort Dix who Jamel had to be concerned about. They had to be outsmarted at every twist and turn, since they were the very people (miserable, locked up, and jealous) who would often jump to conclusions. Anyone of these guys might get the notion, the hint, or the funny idea that Dr. Kay was getting too personal with one prisoner. Then the dime dropping and the investigation would begin.

HARLEM HEAT

By 50 Cent and Mark Anthony

Fast Forward to:
September 2006
Long Island, New York

I can't front. I was nervous as hell.

My heart was thumping a mile a minute, like it was about to jump outta my chest. The same goddamn state trooper had now been following us for more than three exits and I knew that it was just a matter of seconds before he was gonna turn on his lights and pull us over, so I put on my signal and switched lanes and prepared to exit the parkway, hoping that he would change his mind about stopping us.

"Chyna, what the fuck are you doing?" my moms asked me as she fidgeted in her seat.

"Ma, you know this nigga is gonna pull us over, so I'm just acting like I'm purposely exiting before he pulls us over. It'll be easier to play shit off if he does stop us."

"Chyna, I swear to God you gonna get us locked the fuck up. Just relax and drive!" my mother barked as she turned her head to look in the rearview mirror to confirm that the state trooper was still tailing us. She also reached to turn up the volume on the radio and then slumped in her seat a little bit, trying to relax.

Although my moms was trying to play shit cool, the truth was, I knew that she was just as nervous as I was.

"Ma, I already switched lanes, I gotta get off now or we'll look too suspicious," I explained over the loud R. Kelly and Snoop Dogg song that was coming from the speakers.

As soon as I switched lanes and attempted to make my way to the ramp of exit 13, the state trooper threw on his lights, signaling for me to pull over.

"Ain't this a bitch. Chyna, I told yo' ass."

"Ma, just chill," I barked, cutting my mother off. I was panicking and trying to think fast, and the last thing I needed was for my mother to be bitchin' with me.

"I got this. I'ma pull over and talk us outta this. Just follow my lead," I said with my heart pounding as I exited the parkway ramp and made my way on to Linden Boulevard before bringing the car to a complete stop.

I had my foot on the brake and both of my hands on the steering wheel. I inhaled deeply and then exhaled very visibly before putting the car in park. I quickly exited the car, still wearing my Cartier Aviator gold-rimmed shades to help mask my face. The loud R. Kelly chorus continued playing in the background.

"Officer, I'm sorry if I was speeding, but—"

"Miss, step away from the car and put your hands where I can see them," The lone state trooper shouted at me, interrupting my words. He was clutching the nine-millimeter handgun, still in its holster, and he cautiously approached me. Soon, I no longer heard the music coming from the car and I was guessing that my mother had turned it down so that she could try and listen to what the officer was saying.

"Put my hands on the car for what? Let me just explain where I'm going."

The officer wasn't trying to hear it, and he slammed me up against the hood of the car.

"I got a sick baby in the car. What the hell is wrong with you?" I screamed. I was purposely trying to be dramatic while squirming my body and resisting the officer's efforts to pat me down.

On the inside I was still shitting bricks and my heart was still racing a mile a minute. The car was in park at the side of the road and the engine was running idle. I was hoping that my mom would jump into the driver's seat and speed the hell off. There was no sense in both of us getting bagged. And from the looks of things, the aggressive officer didn't seem like he was in the mood for bullshit.

"Is anyone else in the car with you?" the cop asked me as he felt between my legs up to my crotch, checking for a weapon—though he was clearly feeling for more than just a weapon.

My mother's 745 that I was driving had limousine-style tints, and the state trooper couldn't fully see inside the car.

"Just my moms and my sick baby. Yo, on the real, for real, this is crazy. I ain't even do shit and you got me bent over and slammed up against the hood of the car feeling all on my pussy and shit! I got a sick baby that I'm trying to get to the hospital," I yelled while trying to fast-talk the cop. I sucked my teeth and gave him a bunch of eye-rolling and neck-twisting ghetto attitude.

"You didn't do shit? Well if this is a BMW, then tell me why the fuck your plates are registered to a Honda Accord," the six-foot-four-inch drill-sergeant-looking officer screamed back at me.

The cop then reached to open up the driver's door, and just as he pulled the car door open, my moms opened her passenger door. She hadn't taken off the shades or the hat that she had been wearing, and with one foot on the ground and her other foot still inside the car she stood up and asked across the roof of the car if there was a problem.

"Chyna, you okay? What the fuck is going on, Officer?" my mother asked, sounding as if she was highly annoyed.

"Miss, I need you to step away from the car," the officer shouted at my mother.

"Step away from the car for what?" my moms yelled back with even more disgust in her voice.

"Ma, he on some bullshit, I told him that Nina is in the backseat sick as a damn dog and he still on this ol' racist profiling shit."

As soon as I was done saying those words I heard gunfire erupting.

Blaow. Blaow. Blaow. Blaow.

Instinctively I ducked for cover down near the wheel

well, next to the car's twenty-two-inch chrome rims. And when I turned and attempted to see where the shots were coming from, all I saw was the state trooper dropping to the ground. I turned and looked the other way and saw my mom's arms stretched across the roof of the BMW. She was holding her chrome thirty-eight revolver with both hands, ready to squeeze off some more rounds.

"Chyna, you aight?"

"Yeah, I'm good." I shouted back while still half-way crouched down near the tire.

"Well, get your ass in this car and let's bounce!" my moms screamed at me.

I got up off the ground from my kneeling stance and with my high-heeled Bottega Veneta boots I stepped over the bloody state trooper, who wasn't moving. He had been shot point-blank right between the eyes and he didn't look like he was breathing all that well, as blood spilled out of the side of his mouth.

Before I could fully get my ass planted on the cream-colored plush leather driver's seat my mom was hollering for me to hurry up and pull off.

"Drive this bitch, Chyna! I just shot a fucking cop! Drive!"

My mom's frantic yelling had scared my ten month-old baby, who was strapped in her carseat in the back. So with my moms screaming for me to hurry up and drive away from the crime scene and with my startled baby crying and hitting high notes I put the car in drive and I screeched off, leaving the lifeless cop lying dead in the street.

If shit wasn't thick enough for me and my mom already, killing a state trooper had definitely just made things a whole lot thicker. I sped off doing about sixty miles an hour down a quiet residential street in Elmont, Long Island, just off of Linden Boulevard. My heart was thumping and although it was late afternoon on a bright and sunny summer weekday, I was desperately hoping that no eyewitnesses had seen what went down.

BLOW

By 50 Cent
and K'wan

**"The game is not for the faint of heart,
and if you choose to play it,
you better damn well understand the rules."**

Prince sat in the stiff wooden chair totally numb. The tailored Armani suit he had been so proud of when he dropped two grand on it now felt like a straitjacket. He spared a glance at his lawyer who was going over his notes with a worried expression on his face. The young black man had fought the good fight, but in the end it would be in God's hands.

He tried to keep from looking over his shoulder, but he couldn't help it. There was no sign of Sticks, which didn't surprise him. For killing a police officer they were surely going to give him the needle, if he even survived being captured. The police had dragged the river but never found a body. Everyone thought Sticks was dead, but Stone said otherwise. Sticks was his twin, and he would know better than anyone else if he was gone. Prince hoped that Stone was right and wished his friend well wherever fate carried him.

Marisol sat two rows behind him, with Mommy at her side looking every bit of the concerned grandmother. It was hard to believe that she was the embodiment of death, cloaked in kindness. This was the first time he had seen

Mommy since his incarceration, but Marisol had been there every day for the seven weeks the trial had gone on. She tried to stay strong for her man, but he could tell that the ordeal was breaking her down. Cano had sent word through her that he would be taken care of, but Prince didn't want to be taken care of; he wanted to be free.

Keisha sat in the last row, quietly sobbing. She had raised the most hell when the bulls hit, even managing to get herself tossed into jail for obstruction of justice. She had always been a down bitch, and he respected her for it.

Assembled in the courtroom were many faces. Some were friends, but most were people from the neighborhood that just came to be nosey. No matter their motive the sheer number would look good on his part in the eyes of the jury, at least that was what his lawyer had told him. The way the trial seemed to be going, he seriously doubted it at that point.

Lined up to his left were his longtime friends, Daddy-O and Stone. Daddy-O's face was solemn. His dress shirt was pinned up at the shoulder covering the stump where his left arm used to be. It was just one more debt that he owed Diego that he'd never be able to collect on. Stone smirked at a doodling he had done on his legal pad. Prince wasn't sure if he didn't understand the charges they were facing or just didn't care. Knowing Stone, it was probably the latter. He had long ago resigned himself to the fact that he was born into the game and would die in it.

Prince wanted to break down every time he thought how

his run as a boss had ended. To see men that you had grown to love like family take the stand and try to snatch your life to save their own was a feeling that he wouldn't wish on anyone. *No man above the team* was the vow that they had all taken, but in the end only a few kept to it. To the rest, they were just words. They had laughed, cried, smoked weed, and got pussy together, but when the time came to stand like men they laid down like bitches. These men had been like his brothers, but that was before the money came into the picture.

CHAPTER 1
6 months earlier

"**C**ome on Daddy-O, you know me." The young man reminded him, not believing that he'd been turned down. He could already feel the sweat trickling down his back and didn't know how much longer he could hold out.

Daddy-O popped a handful of sunflower seeds in his mouth. He expertly extracted the seed using only his tongue and let the shells tumble around in his mouth until he could feel the salty bite. "My dude, why are you even talking to me about this; holla at my young boy," he nodded at Danny.

"Daddy, you know how this little nigga is; he wouldn't let his mama go for a short, so you know I ain't getting a play."

"Get yo money right and we won't have a problem," Danny told him, and went back to watching the block.

"Listen," the young man turned back to Daddy-O. A thin film of sweat had begun to form on his nose. "All I got is ten dollars on me, but I need at least two to get me to the social security building in the morning. Do me this solid, and I swear I'll get you right when my check comes through."

Daddy-O looked over at Danny, who was giving the kid the once-over. He was short and thin with braids that snaked down the back of his neck. Danny had one of those funny faces. It was kind of like he looked old, but young at the same time . . . if that makes sense.

There was a time when Danny seemed like he had a bright future ahead of him. Though he wasn't the smartest of their little unit, he was a natural at sports. Danny played basketball for Cardinal Hayes High School and was one of the better players on the team. His jump shot needed a little fine-tuning, but he had a mean handle. Danny was notorious for embarrassing his opponents with his wicked crossover. Sports was supposed to be Danny's ticket out, but as most naïve young men did, he chose Hell over Heaven.

For as talented as Danny was physically, he was borderline retarded mentally. Of course not in a literal sense, but his actions made him the most dimwitted of the crew. While his school chums were content to play the roll of gangstas and watch the game from afar, Danny had to be in the thick of it. It was his fascination with the game that caused him to drop out of school in his senior year to pursue his dreams of being a *real nigga*, or a real nigga's sidekick. Danny was a yes-man to the boss, and under the boss is where he would earn his stripes. He didn't really have the heart of a soldier, but he was connected to some stand-up dudes, which provided him with a veil of protection. The hood knew that if you fucked with Danny, you'd have to fuck with his team.

"Give it to him, D," Daddy-O finally said.

Danny looked like he wanted to say something, but a stern look from Daddy-O hushed him. Dipping his hand into the back of his pants, Danny fished around until he found what he was looking for. Grumbling, he handed the young man a small bag of crack.

The young man examined the bag and saw that it was mostly flake and powder. "Man, this ain't nothing but some shake."

"Beggars can't be choosers; take that shit and bounce," Danny spat.

"Yo, shorty you be on some bullshit," the young man said to Danny. There was a hint of anger in his voice, but he knew better than to get stupid. "One day you're gonna have to come from behind Prince and Daddy-O's skirts and handle your own business."

"Go ahead wit that shit, man," Daddy-O said, cracking another seed.

"No disrespect to you, Daddy-O, but shorty got a big mouth. He be coming at niggaz sideways, and it's only on the strength of y'all that nobody ain't rocked him yet."

"Yo, go head wit all that *rocking* shit, niggaz know where I be," Danny said, trying to sound confident. In all truthfulness, he was nervous. He loved the rush of being in the hood with Daddy-O and the team, but didn't care for the bullshit that came with it. Anybody who's ever spent a day on the streets knows that the law of the land more often than not is violence. If you weren't ready to defend your claim, then you needed to be in the house watching UPN.

The young man's eyes burned into Danny's. "Imma see you later," he said, never taking his eyes off Danny as he backed away.

"I'll be right here," Danny said confidently. His voice was deep and stern, but his legs felt like spaghetti. If the kid had rushed him, Danny would have had no idea what to do. He would fight if forced, but it wasn't his first course of action. Only when the kid had disappeared down the path did he finally force himself to relax.

"Punk-ass nigga," Danny said, like he was 'bout that.

"Yo, why you always acting up?" Daddy-O asked.

"What you mean, son?" Danny replied, as if he hadn't just clowned the dude.

"Every time I turn around your ass is in some shit, and that ain't what's up."

Danny sucked his teeth. "Yo, son was trying to stunt on me, B. You know I can't have niggaz coming at my head that way."

"Coming at your head?" Daddy-O raised his eyebrow. "Nigga, he was short two dollars!"

"I'm saying . . ."

"Don't say nothing," Daddy-O cut him off. "We out here trying to get a dollar and you still on your schoolyard bullshit. You need to respect these streets if you gonna get money in them," Daddy-O stormed off leaving Danny there to ponder what he had said.

■

The intense heat from the night before had spilled over to join with the morning sun and punish anyone who didn't have air conditioning, which amounted to damn near the whole hood being outside. That morning the projects were a kaleidoscope of activity. People were drinking, having water fights, and just trying to sit as still as they could in the heat. Grills were set up in front of several buildings, sending smoke signals to the hungry inhabitants.

Daddy-O bopped across the courtyard between 875 and 865. He nodded to a few heads as he passed them, but didn't really stop to chat. It was too damn hot, and being a combination of fat and black made you a target for the sun's taunting rays. A girl wearing boy shorts and a tank-top sat on the bench enjoying an ice-cream cone. She peeked at Daddy-O from behind her pink sunglasses and drew the tip of her tongue across the top of the ice cream.

"Umm, hmm," Daddy-O grumbled, rubbing his large belly. In the way of being attractive, Daddy-O wasn't much to look at. He was a five-eight brute with gorilla-like arms and a jaw that looked to be carved from stone. Cornrows snaked back over his large head and stopped just behind his ears. Though some joked that he had a face that only a mother could love, Daddy-O had swagger. His gear was always up, and he was swift with the gift of gab, earning him points with the ladies.

Everybody in the hood knew Daddy-O. He had lived in the Frederick Douglass Houses for over twelve years at that point. He and his mother had moved there when he was seven years old. Daddy-O had lived a number of places in his life, but no place ever felt like Douglass.

Daddy-O was about to head down the stairs toward 845 when he heard his name being called. He slowed, but didn't stop walking as he turned around. Shambling from 875 in his direction was a crackhead that they all knew as Shakes. She tried to strut in her faded high-heeled shoes, but it ended up as more of a walk-stumble. She was dressed in a black leotard that looked like it was crushing her small breasts. Shakes had been a'ight back in her day, but she didn't get the memo that losing eighty pounds and most of your front teeth killed your sex appeal.

"Daddy-O, let me holla at you for a minute," she half slurred. Shakes's eyes were wide and constantly scanning as if she was expecting someone to jump out on her. She stepped next to Daddy-O and whispered in his ear, "You holding?"

"You know better than that, ma. Go see my little man in the building," he said, in a pleasant tone. Most of the dealers in the neighborhood saw the crackheads as being something less than human and treated them as such, but not Daddy-O. Having watched his older brother and several of his other relatives succumb to one drug or another, Daddy-O understood it better than most. Cocaine and heroin were the elite of their line. Boy and Girl, as they were sometimes called, were God and Goddess to those foolish enough to be enticed by their lies. They had had the highest addiction rate, and the most cases of relapses. Daddy-O had learned early that a well-known crackhead could be more valuable to you than a member of your team, if you knew how to use them.

"A'ight, baby, that's what it is," she turned to walk away and almost lost her balance. In true crackhead form, she righted herself and tried to strut even harder. "You need to call a sista sometime," she called over her shoulder.

Daddy-O shook his head. There wasn't a damn thing he could call Shakes but what she was, a corpse that didn't know it was dead yet. Daddy-O continued down the stairs and past the small playground. A group of kids were dancing around in the elephant-shaped sprinkler tossing water on each other. One of them ran up on Daddy-O with a half-filled bowl, but a quick threat of an ass whipping sent the kid back to douse one of his friends with the water. Stopping to exchange greetings with a Puerto Rican girl he knew, Daddy-O disappeared inside the bowels of 845.

HEAVEN'S FURY

By 50 Cent and Meta Smith

PROLOGUE

Here Comes the Bride

December 2002, St. Michael the Archangel Catholic Church, Chicago

he bride looked beautiful in her traditional white gown. She twirled in the mirror and grinned at her reflection. She didn't want to seem vain, but she did look really beautiful. She couldn't believe that her wedding day had finally arrived. It was the happiest day of her life. Her mother and grandmother cried tears of joy and the ceremony hadn't even begun; they were just so touched at the pure beauty before them.

"I remember my wedding day," the bride's mother said. "I was so nervous."

"I'm not nervous at all," the bride replied. "I'm too happy to be nervous."

"No jitters about the wedding night?" the grandmother asked with a wicked grin. "Life as a married woman has its . . . duties."

"Abuelita!" the bride said with a giggle. "I'm not nervous about *that*, either."

The grandmother put her hand over her heart. "*Dios mío! Please* tell me that you're not . . . experienced!" The bride's mother and grandmother both waited for her reply. The bride smiled cryptically but didn't answer, and the women's eyes grew wide with shock. Unable to control herself, the bride erupted in a fit of giggles.

"Relax, Abuela. Relax, Mami. I'm pure as the driven snow. I just couldn't help teasing you a little."

"Don't play with us like that," the bride's mother replied, exhaling in relief.

"You know how important it is to God to remain a virgin until you're married," her grandmother said.

"I do."

"And Ricardo, he never pressured you to go all the way?" her mother asked.

"No, Mami. He's a good man. The best," the bride said. "I'm so lucky. Most guys would never have understood how important my faith is to me, but not my Rico. He respects the fact that I'm a virgin. In fact, he told me that he loved me *more* because I was one."

The mother and grandmother of the bride smiled at each other, filled with pride. They'd raised their little girl in the

Church, and she didn't stray. That was a difficult feat to achieve in the twenty-first century.

The bride's grandmother took a string of pearls from around her neck and placed them around the bride's.

"Abuela—" the bride began. Her grandmother silenced her.

"*Sí*, your *abuelo* gave me these and now I am giving them to you."

"You're gonna ruin my makeup," the bride protested as her eyes welled with tears.

"You're so beautiful you don't need it," the bride's mother said, complimenting her only child.

The bride smiled at her mother and grandmother and then drew them both into her arms for a group hug.

"I love you guys so much," she said. "Now get outta here and get into the chapel so I can get married already!" They all laughed and the mother and grandmother left. Then the bride pulled her rosary from her handbag and closed her eyes. She recited the traditional Catholic prayer she'd memorized just for this occasion.

"O Jesus, lover of the young, the dearest friend I have, in all confidence I open my heart to You to beg Your light and assistance in the important task of planning my future. Give me the light of Your grace, that I may decide wisely concerning the person who is to be my partner through life. Dearest Jesus, send me such a one whom in Your divine wisdom You judge best suited to be united with me in marriage.

May his character reflect some of the traits of Your own sacred heart. May he be upright, loyal, pure, sincere, and noble, so that with united efforts and with pure and unselfish love we both may strive to perfect ourselves in soul and body, as well as the children it may please You to entrust to our care. Bless our friendship before marriage, that sin may have no part in it. May our mutual love bind us so closely that our future home may ever be most like Your own at Nazareth.

"O Mary Immaculate, sweet mother of the young, to your special care I entrust the decision I am to make as to my future husband. You are my guiding star! Direct me to the person with whom I can best cooperate in doing God's holy will, with whom I can live in peace, love, and harmony in this life and attain eternal joys in the next. Amen."

The bride opened her eyes, confident that God would answer her prayers. He always did. In fact, He already had. After all, He'd sent her the most perfect man in the world, the love of her life, her soul mate. Now they were about to be joined in holy matrimony. It was every woman's dream.

The bride could barely contain her elation at the fact that out of all the people in the world, she'd met her perfect match. Her groom-to-be was handsome, ambitious, and he adored her and treated her like a queen. He loved her for who she was on the inside, not just for her body, and she knew that was a real blessing. She was a lucky girl indeed.

The bride smoothed out her full hoopskirt made of heavy beaded silk and twirled giddily. Then taking one last look in the mirror, she pulled her crystal-encrusted veil over her face and prepared to take the biggest step of her life.

CHAPTER 1

The Life

April 2007, Chicago

As the sun rose above the icy waters of Lake Michigan and sunlight began to stream through the blinds of a luxury high-rise apartment, Ricardo Diaz rolled over in the large silk-sheeted bed he occupied and grabbed a handful of his bedmate's ample bosom. He squeezed the firm golden mounds, tweaking the hardening dark nipples until the woman lying next to him stirred and moaned. Ricardo's hands began to travel down her abdomen until he reached her box and opened it. His fingers moved expertly, flicking her pleasure button until her juices began to flow. Without saying a word, Ricardo inserted his rock-hard manhood into the woman and began to thrust slowly in and out of her wet sweetness.

"*Ay*, Papi," the woman moaned, thrusting her hips against him in perfect harmony.

"That's right, girl," Ricardo said, encouraging his lover, pumping faster.

He fondled the woman's breasts and played with her engorged clitoris until he could feel her walls contract around his hardness and she shuddered and shivered with delight. Ricardo loved the way it felt when a woman came for him. There was nothing on earth like it, the high was incomparable, except for the high he got when he was making money. New pussy and new money were things that made life sweet for a baller like Ricardo Diaz and he had plenty of both.

Engulfed in the warm and throbbing sexy *mami* he was piping, Ricardo felt like a king. He always felt like a king when he was with *her*. She was his fly bitch, his *mami chula*, and not only was she fine but she was a freak.

"You like that?" Ricardo asked as he felt his lover climax again. "Come for me, Chula."

"Ooh, I'm coming for you, Papi," the woman squealed with pleasure.

Once he was convinced that his lover was satisfied, Ricardo went for his, grabbing a handful of the woman's hair and pounding her so hard that the sound of their skin slapping against each other echoed through the room like claps of thunder. Ricardo grunted and with a few final thrusts he climaxed deep within the woman, who sighed happily. Spent, Ricardo removed himself from the woman and rolled over onto his back, breathing heavily.

"Go fix me some breakfast, Gloria," Ricardo commanded, and his lady friend did as she was told. Minutes later, she returned with a cup of freshly squeezed orange juice and a cup of coffee.

"Will Belgian waffles be okay?" she asked.

"Yeah. Lots of butter, syrup, and powdered sugar."

"I'll fix them just the way you like them, Papi," she replied and went to prepare the meal.

Ricardo stretched lazily and propped his hands behind his head after clicking on the forty-two-inch plasma-screen television mounted on the bedroom wall. He went over all the things he had to do that day in his mind. After he left his Chula, he'd head to his business and make a few stacks, then he'd roll through the streets and check a couple of traps. Somewhere along the way he'd put in a call to his wife; maybe he'd take her out later to dinner and a show. But not before he got breakfast in bed and some head from his side lady, who'd returned to the bedroom with a tray of steaming-hot food. But the food would have to wait. As if she'd read his mind, Ricardo's *mami chula* climbed back into the bed and snuggled beneath the sheets, taking his manhood into her mouth and having a little breakfast of her own.

This is the life, Ricardo thought to himself as he received the blow job of a lifetime.

Heaven Diaz rolled over in bed to find her husband's side empty. Again. It was the second time in a week that her husband hadn't made it home. Her intuition told her that he was unfaithful, but she willed herself to believe the excuses he fed her. *Ricardo loves me and he's working hard to build and maintain the wonderful life I have,* she often told herself.

She got out of bed and went down the stairs of her five-thousand-square-foot home and into the kitchen. She couldn't help but marvel at the kitchen fit for a chef with its stainless-steel appliances and copper pots. Heaven had every gadget and gizmo known to the culinary world, and prepared meals fit for royalty every night of the week, but her husband was rarely home to enjoy them. When she first got married she thought that there would be candlelight and champagne every night, but her childhood fantasy was quickly marred by reality. Ricardo was a workaholic and put in long hours on the job as the owner of an exotic car sales, rental, and driver service.

But Heaven definitely reaped the rewards of her husband's labor. The fabulous kitchen where she whipped up meals was inside a tight, custom-built crib nestled near the shores of Lake Michigan in the Hyde Park section of Chicago. There were six bedrooms, seven and a half baths, and an indoor swimming pool in the four-story manse. Ricardo had given Heaven carte blanche when meeting with the architect who designed the home. They spared no expense when deciding what fixtures the home would have, and it was even featured in the real estate sections of the major Chicago newspapers and in home and architecture magazines.

Heaven also had the wardrobe of a queen; every garment in her closet sported a designer label. She had more shoes than Carrie Bradshaw and Imelda Marcos combined, and she had more bling than a diamond mine in Sierra Leone. Heaven drove the exotic car of her choice and switched whips whenever the whim hit. Over the past year she'd pushed a Rover, a Lambo, a Ferrari, and a Maserati. And on the rare occasions she didn't feel like driving, she had a fleet of drivers at her disposal.

She had everything that any woman could want and then some. She had everything but her husband's time, but without sacrifice one can't attain one's goals, or at least that was Heaven's rationale. One day soon, her husband would have the time to spend with her that she craved, and maybe they could even start a family. But until then, she'd have to be resigned to living in the satisfying lap of luxury, even if it was a lonely position.

Aside from perpetual loneliness, Heaven suffered from another nagging problem. She had her doubts as to where all the material things her husband lavished on her came from. Her gut told her that something was amiss. She knew that her husband made a good living and worked extremely hard; in fact, she'd helped her husband attain much of the success that he had. Heaven made a million phone calls and put in countless hours of legwork helping her husband get his business off the ground and over the years the company flourished. But Heaven had her suspicions because little by little certain things weren't adding up.

For starters, there were the late nights, no-shows, and suspicious phone calls that Rico got all hours of the night when he did find his way home. He'd have brief, stilted conversations with whoever was on the other end. Heaven would ask her husband about those things, but his excuses always left her with far more questions than answers. Then there was the abundance of cash he always seemed to have. Most men never had more than a few hundred bucks on them, but Rico traveled with wads and wads of dough that made Heaven fear that he'd be the target of a robbery sooner or later. She told him that most businessmen used credit and that he should do the same and simply pay the bills on time, but Ricardo assured her that he knew what he was doing.

There was also the fact that they lived a lifestyle more

suited to an athlete or some other celebrity and not a business-man; businessmen were usually far more understated. Ricardo and Heaven's assets were worth millions of dollars. And Ricardo never seemed to care about how much anything cost; he just bought what he wanted when he wanted. An entrepreneur usually had to be a bit more frugal and cost-conscious. But when Heaven suggested that they stack more money for a rainy day Rico balked. He told her that they had more money than they could ever spend in one lifetime and that the future held no financial worries, but his cavalier attitude only made Heaven worry more. She was concerned that perhaps her husband had been tempted by the lure of the streets.

Heaven was sweet but she wasn't stupid. She'd seen more than her share of hustlers and dope boys growing up in the tough Logan Square neighborhood of Chicago. And plenty of them had tried to win her affection but she wanted no part of that kind of life. She enjoyed glitz and glamour but was wise enough to know that material things could never be the measure of a man. And she believed that drugs were poison that were killing the masses and making the world a worse place while a select few profited. But Heaven knew that such temptations weren't always easy for a man to walk away from, and she shuddered at the mere thought that her husband could be involved in illegal activity and prayed that he wasn't so stupid or greedy. She'd been bold enough to confront Ricardo a time or two about her feelings, but he always had an explanation that made sense and Heaven had been raised to trust her husband. After all, if she couldn't trust him, what was the point of being married?

Heaven tried not to sweat her suspicions. After all, she was a child of God, and He would always look after her. And Heaven firmly believed that what was done in the dark would always come to light and the truth—if it was anything other than what her husband told her—would be revealed in due time.

Heaven sighed as she prepared to begin her day. *Flaws, worries, and all this is my life*, Heaven said to herself.

Gloria Cruz sucked Ricardo's cock for what felt like an hour. Her jaw had a cramp and her mouth was becoming dry but that didn't curb her enthusiasm. She slurped and sucked loudly, moaning and groaning and looking up at Ricardo like he was the don of all dons. She flickered her tongue over the head of his penis and blew lightly over it before deep throating the length. Ricardo grabbed her by the hair and grunted before spurting inside of her mouth, and Gloria hungrily devoured every drop.

"I love you, Papi," she said, looking up at him with a smile on her face and sincerity in her eyes.

Gloria was crazy for Ricardo, she always had been. They'd dated off and on from the time they were twelve. She'd gone to college and they maintained their relationship until Gloria got a fellowship to study dance in Paris that she couldn't pass up. Dancing was her passion and she had the opportunity of a lifetime to follow her dream. They promised to stay together but the distance made things difficult and then Ricardo met Heaven. He'd fallen head over heels and within the space of six months they were married.

Ricardo had claimed it was an impulse, that he'd missed Gloria so much that he tried to duplicate their relationship with someone else. He claimed it was Gloria who was the love of his life, and that marrying Heaven had been a big mistake. The fact that Ricardo had moved on so quickly broke her heart and she vowed never to speak to him again, but when she returned stateside four years later they ran into each other at a party and reignited their old flame. Gloria had never stopped loving Ricardo, and she wouldn't let him go again, even if it meant that she had to share him. The way she saw it, Ricardo was her man, and Heaven was just on borrowed time.

"I love you, too, baby," Ricardo told her, and it was the truth. He did love Gloria. He'd always loved Gloria. He just loved his wife more. When he met Heaven he knew that she was something special. Heaven was breathtakingly beautiful. Her golden skin, sparkling dark eyes, and thick luxurious hair had him enraptured immediately, and when he got to know her he knew that she would be the perfect wife.

Heaven was virginal and sweet and never gave him any problems. His relationship with Gloria had thrived on drama, heat, and intensity. Heaven trusted him blindly and was devoted and true. Gloria had been suspicious and accused him of cheating all the time. Heaven helped him with his business when it was first starting out and Ricardo knew that she would lay down her life for him. Gloria was just as committed to handling her business as he was, and Ricardo loved her hustle. But he didn't want to marry a hustler. His wife had to be all about him 24/7/365 and he had that in Heaven.

"Baby, why can't we be together?" Gloria asked him.

"We've been over this a million times. I'm married to Heaven. She's a good woman, she doesn't deserve me walking out on her."

"If she's such a good woman, why are you with me half the week?" Gloria asked him. "And do you think that I deserve to play second fiddle to her?"

"You're not second fiddle. You're a good woman, too, and I care about you and want to be with you. But you know and I know that I need a woman who is all about me. I need my wife to take care of my needs."

"I do take care of your needs," Gloria snapped. She resented it when Ricardo acted as if Heaven did something for him that she didn't.

"I need my wife to put me before herself," Ricardo said. Gloria stayed silent. "That's what I thought," he told her. "Besides, Heaven is more Catholic than the pope. She'd never give me a divorce. Now, Chula, let's not talk about this, okay? I love you, and that's all that matters. I have to go to work." Ricardo got up to take a shower while Gloria flopped on the bed, crossed her arms in front of her chest, and pouted. Ricardo reached into the pocket of the pants he'd been wearing the night before and pulled out a bankroll.

"I've got something that will make you feel better," Ricardo told Gloria, tossing her the wad of cash that was bound by a thick green rubber band. "I've got to roll down to Miami to pick up a car for my personal collection. I want you to come with me. So go buy yourself some fly shit. I want you to be the sexiest bitch on the beach. If you need more, hit me on the hip and I got you."

Gloria grinned, thumbing through the stack of bills. There was a couple thousand dollars there. She'd definitely need more, but this was a good start. Ricardo went to take his shower and Gloria went to clean the kitchen. Suddenly, a wave of nausea hit her like a tsunami, causing her to run to the second bathroom of her penthouse apartment and heave into the toilet. Gloria emptied the contents of her stomach into the bowl and then flushed. She rinsed her mouth out with some water and mouthwash and then stared at her reflection in the mirror.

Gloria smiled when she realized that her period was a couple of days late. She knew in her gut that she was pregnant. Now she had the perfect ammunition against her nemesis Heaven, and it was growing inside of her. Ricardo would never turn his back on his child. Never. And Gloria was hoping that Heaven was the type of woman who would put up with a lot of shit, but not an outside child. That would be grounds for her to get an annulment. Then she and Ricardo could be together forever, the way it was intended.

It's going to be the life, Gloria mused.